THE TAKER

BY J. M. Steele

HYPERION / NEW YORK

**For those whom I love
(You know who you are)**

● ● ● ● ● ● ● ● ● ● ● ● ● ● ● ● ● ● ● ●

First Edition
10 9 8 7 6 5 4 3 2 1
Designed by Elizabeth H. Clark
Printed in the United States of America
This book is set in 12.5-Point Baskerville.
Library of Congress Cataloging-in-Publication Data on file.
ISBN 0-7868-4930-4
Reinforced binding

Visit www.hyperionbooksforchildren.com

> **Please complete the following sentence with the best possible word choices.**

If Carly were to _____ the SAT, she would be _____ for life.

   (A) ace . . . set
   (B) miss . . . humiliated
   (C) fail . . . home
   (D) eat . . . sick
   (E) blow . . . screwed

SO THERE I WAS—perched on the edge of my bed with my finger already on the speed dial. This was it. My date with destiny.

But destiny had to wait another five minutes.

It was only 7:55 A.M.

If you were a high school senior anywhere in the

country that day, you were doing the same thing I was doing—that classic rite of initiation that would determine what your future would hold . . . where you would go to college . . . who your friends would be . . . what kind of job you'd get. I was, of course . . . waiting to get my SAT scores.

Mr. Biggles dozed belly-up on my shag carpet, totally oblivious to what was about to unfold (unlike my mother, who I could hear doing her pathetic ab-blaster routine downstairs in the den). Even my fingers drumming on the bedside table failed to rouse him from his puppy dream world.

"I'm glad *you're* so blasé about all this."

Okay—so I was tense. But isn't everyone when it comes time to get his or her SAT scores? Jen and I had talked about calling the College Board together that morning—shouldn't best friends always be there for each other?—but in the end we decided it was smartest just to do it on our own and then text each other after. And I was glad. Best friends or not—I couldn't deal with the thought of seeing anyone right then. I was a stress case.

7:56 A.M.

I reminded myself that it was ridiculous to be so nervous. I mean, when I took the test two weeks before, I'd felt really good about how it had gone. I'd finished with plenty of time, I'd only really got stuck on like, a handful of hard math questions, and as for the essays—*hel-lo*, I'm a *writer*—it was cake. But for some reason, there was a huge pit in the bottom of my stomach. It hadn't helped of course that the night before, my ever-nurturing and supportive father pointed out that if I "bombed"—his word, not mine!—I'd only have eight weeks to study again for the last SAT test date that would count for college applications.

7:57 A.M.

College. I could feel my mind begin to accelerate. If I did poorly on the SAT, then I'd never get into Princeton. And if I didn't get into Princeton, I wouldn't be able to study creative writing with Toni Morrison. And if I didn't study creative writing with Toni Morrison, I'd end up being one of those hack writers who spits out obituaries for some jerkwater newspaper while trying to get their short story published in some minor literary journal printed in . . .

Shut up, Carly, I said to myself.

7:58 A.M.

This had happened before. Sometimes—and I don't really like to admit this—I could get pretty wound up. I mean, if you saw me you'd never know it, but it's true. And it always happened during big tests like the SAT, because let's face it—it wasn't just about my writing. It was about what my father expected for me—Joe Princeton, Class of '74. About Brad and me staying together—Princeton's lacrosse team was practically falling all over themselves to get him to play for the Tigers. And it was also about what my mother always liked to call "living up to my potential." Whatever that meant. So when I looked at all those bubbles, it was like my brain shut down.

Analysis: Carly freaks out during standardized testing!

7:59 A.M.

Just relax.

In an effort to distract myself, I picked up the Magic 8-Ball that Jen had given me for my thirteenth birthday and shook it.

"Will I ace the SAT?" I asked out loud. Mr. Biggles lifted his head, and for once appeared at least passably interested in the answer.

The ball was blurry for a moment before settling on: *TOO SOON TO TELL.*

Of course.

I tossed it back on the bed.

As my score was apparently still up in the air—and despite the fact that my shadow hadn't darkened the doorstep of a church since I was confirmed four years previous—I pressed my hands together and said a quick prayer for a perfect score. Truly, only the Big Man upstairs could change things now.

8:00 A.M.

Here we go.

I rose to my feet and hit speed dial. Somewhat suspiciously, the sounds from my mother working out downstairs ceased. I guess she'd had her eye on the clock, too.

"Thank you for calling the College Board," a recorded voice answered. "If you are a student, press one. If . . ." I punched one with all my pent-up energy and nearly broke my finger.

Then I punched in my ID and PIN numbers. Surprisingly, the closer I got to getting my scores, the more confident I became that it was all going to work out. Not that I was going to get a perfect score, mind you, but let's just say I began to feel certain that the Fates had prepared a place for me in the Valhalla that was the 96th percentile or higher.

Princeton, here I come.

"Your scores are as follows," the automated voice began. "Writing . . . 710."

I am a genius.

"Critical Reading . . . 510."

Um—what?

"Math . . . 490."

Oh. My. God.

Something was wrong. Something was very wrong. There had to be an explanation. I must've typed in the wrong student ID number. Yes—that was definitely it!

I hung up, redialed, and went through the commands again.

"Writing 710. Critical Reading 510. Math 490."

OMG. This was a disaster even the Man upstairs couldn't undo. How would I face my parents? My friends? Brad? I couldn't even bring myself to look at Mr. Biggles.

I heard my cell beep and saw there was a text from Jen.

JEN: 700. 660. 650!!!! How r urs?

How was it that I had become the sacrificial lamb to the SAT gods? 710 was great, of course, but 510 and 490? That was a total car crash.

I texted my dismal scores back to Jen, but by now I felt tears forming in my eyes, and I had to do everything I could to keep myself from bursting into sobs. This just didn't make any sense. I was a good student. I was considered the smart one among my friends—and in my class, for that matter. How could I have eaten it so hard on the SAT?

Images of what my future held formed in my mind. A lame junior college. Brad taking up with some Ivy League ice queen while I was reduced to dating a Domino's delivery boy. Dying alone and penniless in some rent-controlled apartment in the Bronx—or worse—dying alone still living with my parents!

My phone beeped again with another text, and while I couldn't handle seeing another person's stellar test scores, for some reason I picked it up anyway. It was from a restricted number. As Brad, my boyfriend, was the only person I knew with a restricted number, I opened the flashing envelope icon.

CALLER UNKNOWN: I CAN HELP YOU.

I squinted and stared at the phone.

I can help you?

Almost unconsciously, I looked around and out my window—feeling suddenly as if I were being watched. There was no one there.

I scrolled down on the message, expecting more, but that's all it said. There was, however, a signature.

-The Taker

When Carly's parents find out that she bombed the SAT, they will _____ and _____.

    (A) shrug their shoulders ... tell her they love her anyway

    (B) vomit ... beat her

    (C) have a heart attack ... die

    (D) smile ... raise her allowance

    (E) weep ... ask themselves why they didn't have a
        second child

TWO MINUTES LATER, I'd come to the conclusion that the text from "the Taker" was just a hoax. It was probably some pathetic loser getting his rocks off by messing with me. I mean, *the Taker*? As in, that person who we've all heard about who will take your SAT for you and get you a really good score? Please. He (or she!) didn't really exist. That was just a story people made up. So I told myself to put it out of my mind, and that's exactly what I did. Besides, I had a bigger issue to deal with—namely how I was going to get out of the house without seeing the 'rents.

You see, I needed to bolt from my house without telling my parents my scores—cowardly, maybe—but how could I break it to Dad that his only heir wasn't going to Princeton? Since putting on my first Tigers onesy that fateful day in the delivery room, the pressure has been relentless—relentless in a way only "good" parents can be. Check the photo album if you don't believe me: me in Princeton hats, me in Princeton scarves, me in Princeton mittens or sweatshirts or basketball tanks or sweaters, T-shirts, shorts, shorts in orange, shorts in black, shorts with tigers on the ass. Lately, it was slinky tanks and girl boxers. You name it. I owned it.

So did I have choice? For all you Monday morning quarterbacks out there . . . let's see . . . um . . . I could've broken the news to them over breakfast and watched as my mother sobbed into her coffee and my father just shook his head and muttered to himself, "What did I do wrong, what did I do wrong?"

But I think not.

Or maybe you think I should've left a note. Perhaps something along the lines of . . .

> Dear Mom and Dad,
> Just checked my SAT scores, and I think
> we should stick a Colchester Community
> College sticker above the Princeton one.
> No rush, but just something to keep in the
> back of your minds.
> Sincerely,
> Carly the Failure

No, that was not an option, either.

Besides, the way I saw it, there was a ninety-nine percent chance Mom would just call for my scores the moment she found out I had left the house without telling her. Actually, that was my plan. If she did, and I knew she would, I'd have what I like to call "self-righteous outrage" on my side, and nothing heals wounds faster than self-righteous outrage.

If my plan went correctly, it would all unfold something like this:

1. I walk in the door after school. Mom admits calling the College Board.

2. My mouth drops open and I make a face that could only mean "How could you . . ."
3. Moments later, I shed tears without words (this inevitably has a devastating effect on the parent).
4. Finally, I feign indignation and shout, "I can't believe you would go behind my back like that. . . ." and run to my room.
5. Case closed.

Yes, by the time self-righteous outrage was in full effect, my dismal SAT scores would seem like a minor hiccup on a distant horizon for my parents.

Bottom line, here was the non-SAT math: Avoid Immediate Stress + Future Self-Righteous Outrage = Bolting. Bolting was the right answer.

By this point I was already out the back door and down the driveway, where I sat on the curb waiting for Molly, my other bf since seventh grade. Most mornings Molly swung by around 8:00, and we would make a mad sprint to 'bucks and get some foamy capps with caramel before making our way to Room 363. Actually she was practically always late, hair wet, putting makeup on, and driving a little too fast for her—and later, our—own good. Death defying or not, it was my favorite part of every day. Just girl talk without the bitchy pressure that comes once you were inside the prison walls of Guilford High School.

Today, the best thing about Molly was that she couldn't give a rat's ass about the SAT. Nope, Molly's master plan was to be on the first train to New York right after graduation. You guessed it—she is (or I should say, wants to be) an actress. But she's more than that, too, because—let's face it—a lot of actresses are a bit flaky. No, Molly is confident and wise, sort of like she's lived a couple lives before this one. Now, I wouldn't say she's book smart. But as she likes to say, "I ain't got a mind for figures, but I stills got something up here." (Please add fake heavy southern twang.)

It was already 8:10, and when Molly was this late, it meant I had to chat with Ronald Gross (pronounced like floss, as his mother is quick to say). Of course, I don't have to tell you that in middle school, his name was just "Gross," like you'd think it sounds.

Ronald Gross was one of those poor souls who couldn't find a fellow senior to drive him to school and had no car of his own. For Ronald that spelled, of course, School Bus, and nothing shouts freak like taking the bus when you're eighteen years old. Even freshmen don't respect you. His bus came at 8:15—it had a staggered route, so the same bus picked up the hicks from North Guilford first, dropped them off at school, and then did a quick swing around the Guilford Green and picked up the few sad stragglers whose parents wouldn't drive them. Hence the 8:15 pick-up time.

Talking with Ronald was always awkward—we usually shouted across the street—and more often than not he stared at his shoes and mumbled a lot.

"Hey," he said, kicking some pebbles against the curb. He walked up to me and lifted his chin. "The bus comes on this side of the street now."

"Oh, really . . . huh . . . Big change," I answered, wondering why he thought I'd care.

I couldn't actually remember seeing Ronald this up close. He had a boyish face. No beard, not even peach fuzz on his lip, and I speculated that he probably hadn't even passed through puberty yet. He sported an enormous backpack—no doubt filled with Dungeons & Dragons gear—and was wearing the same type of sunglasses my dad wore, in like, the 90s.

"What's that you're reading?" I asked.

"*All the President's Men.* It's for Mr. Devaney's class."

"Oh, I hear he's great."

Ronald mumbled something I couldn't understand, something about Devaney and Marx and beards.

Freak.

Silence again. Somewhere a dog barked down the street.

Although talking to Ronald was tough, I generally managed. Today was more awkward than usual, however, because the other notable fact about Ronald Gross that I should disclose is that he is one of four members of the 2400 Club at good old Guilford High School.

Ah, the 2400 Club. What might that be, you ask? Being in the 2400 Club means that you scored in the top one percent of the country on the SAT. The ultimate honor for every brainiac geek who ever wandered the hallways of John Doe HS, Dorkville, USA. Don't get me wrong, I'm not putting them down. No. My bitterness derives from pure jealousy. I'm not a member, not even close. After today, I felt lucky not to be in the 1200 Club.

None of *my* friends—I'm relieved to admit—are members of the 2400 Club, not even my luv, Brad, though something tells me he could be if he weren't so busy being wonderful at everything else.

But I digress—more about him later.

I was the one who had made up the name with Jen,

who is the editor of the school paper. She was doing an article on kids from our school who had crushed the SAT, and she'd needed a headline. I said, "Call it the 2400 Club"—and it stuck. When the article ran, beneath the headline was a picture of the current members in our school: Mary "Bookworm" Bookman, Yang Ling, Ed Rice and . . . of course . . . Ronald Gross.

Mary Bookman—member Number One—worked in the library and was a social pariah of the highest order. Though she always scored well above the curve, she possessed zero emotional intelligence and wouldn't even look at you when you spoke to her. Schoolwide infamy for her lay in the fact that, in the sixth grade, she'd picked her nose and ate what she'd found—an event witnessed and later much publicized by Billy Barnes. That, of course, was a certain death card you just couldn't escape until you reached college—if you were even that lucky. Mom told me she suspected Mary was the kind of girl who would blossom in college and come home a chic lesbian, but I was never quite sure what that was. Chic lesbian? Like Ellen?

Member number two—Yang Ling. Ding-a-Ling (as the jerks on the football team referred to him) didn't speak English very well, but he'd scored perfectly on the math portion. Jen had given him 2400 status based on the fact that everyone agreed that if he hadn't grown up in Hunan Province, China, he would've been the first person to have scored a 2500.

Member number three was Ed Rice. Simply put, Ed Rice is the smartest person I'd ever met. Preternaturally brilliant, in all the AP courses, summer math classes at Columbia. Oh, and he's thirteen.

And then there is Ronald. Compared to the other three, he is James Dean, but on the normal-like-the-rest-of-the-world scale, he is a bit of a geek. Captain of the chess club, member of the debate team, runner (sort of) for the JV cross-country team—you get the picture. Other social fouls include being the tutoring lab coordinator and still delivering the *New Haven Register* after school. But he isn't *that* bad, I suppose—just totally clueless. An older sister or something might have given him a prayer.

"So, how'd ya do?" he eventually asked.

I pretended like I didn't know what he was talking about. "On what?"

"On the SAT?"

"Oh, right!" I beamed my best fake smile. "Fine. I did fine."

I guess he saw right through me, because he shifted his weight and bent over to pick a dandelion. He blew at it.

"Yeah, I hate tests, too."

My back stiffened. Was I wrong, or was that a pity play on his part—he hates tests, too!

"Still can't find a ride, huh?"

I know—I was cruel. Straight to Hell. But I was annoyed that some Grade A dork was trying to give me sympathy.

"It's the same," he said, tossing the dandelion into the gutter and shoving his hands in his pockets. "It's brutal."

He sighed and looked up at the sky.

Okay, now I felt like a bit of a jerk. Maybe he was being nice and saying those things to make me feel better. And there I was rubbing his school bus–taking nose in the dirt.

"Hey, isn't that Molly?" he said.

An instant later, Molly came roaring up in her white Mustang—a '74 her dad had rebuilt for her—and screeched to a halt.

"Let's go, girl!" she shouted.

Relieved to be able to eject from my awkward situation with Ronald, I waved good-bye and jumped into Molly's car. She hit the gas and we took off.

"C-C?" Molly grinned. It was our code term for when we made nice with "shy" boys. Translation: charity conversation.

"Totally," I answered, rolling my eyes. "Check me off for my good deed for the week!"

But before we turned off my street, for some reason I looked in the side-view mirror back at Ronald. As the school bus pulled up, he sort of hit himself in the head like he was annoyed at something he'd said, and moments later some freshman was hanging out the window shouting something at him. I could see the boy's mouth forming the words, "Gross, Gross, Gross." Sadly, I knew it sounded exactly as you might imagine.

But I had my own problems to worry about.

SURVIVING THE SAT: TIP #1

HOW TO DEAL
AFTER YOU GET YOUR SCORES BACK

● ●

If you find out you blew it on the SAT, under no circumstances should you go to school that day. Take a sick day,
fake a grandparent's illness, or throw yourself in front of
a car. Just don't go.

Trust me!

BY THE TIME I'd reached the hallway where my locker is, Mr. Claflin was already closing the homeroom door. I considered briefly begging him to let me in without a late, but soon realized that it would be hopeless. He was one of those teachers who actually relished closing doors, marking students late, and handing out detentions—you know the type. I despised him, and he despised me. Luckily, it was only my fourth late, and you needed five for an in-school suspension—but now, I reminded myself, there was no more pushing it. If I got an in-school for being late, my parents would make me take the bus. And we know what that would mean: a semester-long date with Ronald Gross every morning.

But when I arrived at my locker I stopped cold.

There was a folded note sticking out of the grille.

Odd. And, much as I tried to convince myself it was a hoax, I immediately found myself wondering if it was from the Taker—or whoever had sent me that text earlier in the day. For the second time that morning, I felt my heart accelerate. Was I being stalked?

I pulled out the note and glanced around the pretty-much empty hallway. I opened it.

I breathed a sigh of relief. Well, sort of. It wasn't from the Taker. It was from my college adviser, Mrs. G. She wanted to see me after sixth period. I guess she wanted to find out how my SAT scores were.

Great.

Popping my locker door open, I dug through all my stuff inside this 12- by 36-inch sliver of a box, in search of my eye makeup. Besides the obvious books, pencils, etc. that my locker held, it also had my in-school makeup bag, complete with lipstick, brushes, and emergency tampons. More important, there was a photo of Brad surfing big waves in California—so sexy—and a picture of us at the Junior Prom (and we looked fab, if I do say so myself!). Beneath my mini-Brad shrine was a photo of me, Molly, and Jen from our school trip to New York last year, with *The Sistas of Luv* scrawled beneath it. Spacious and totally private it was not, but I cherished those moments at my locker in the beginning of the day. It was like my home away from home, and it let me get centered before having to deal with the backstabbing and nail-biting that was a day at GHS.

"Hey, babe," I heard, before an arm with a yellow LIVE STRONG bracelet hugged me from behind.

It was Brad.

"Hiya," I said, turning around. He gave me a big kiss on the lips.

Mmmmm. Now that was how I liked to start the day.

"I left you a message last night, but you didn't call me back," I said, still nose to nose.

"Yeah—sorry," he replied, breaking away. "I was hanging out with Rick and lost track of the time."

Brad was notoriously bad about returning calls and remembering plans, but having dated him for over a year now, I had to learn to live with it. Or at least that's how he'd put it.

"Oh, okay," I said, neither here nor there. Much as I didn't want to get into the SAT convo, I couldn't help myself. "How'd you do?"

He shrugged his shoulders with nonchalance. "2190. You?"

No. Way. 2190? He got a 2190?! I loved Brad, but was there no justice in the world? I don't think he'd even opened a study book!

"Wow," I managed to get out. But my feelings of indignation quickly shifted to fear. If Brad got a 2190, how could I tell him how badly I'd done? He'd think I was stupid. That I wasn't good enough for him. He'd leave me.

"Not that well," I started. "Not too well at all."

"That can't be," he said. "I'm sure you're just being too hard on yourself. I'm sure you did great."

"I'm serious, Brad."

"Oh, c'mon. Whadja get?"

I took a breath.

"1710."

He leaned forward and turned his ear as if he hadn't heard me right. "What did you say?"

"I got a 1710!" I said, a little louder than I would've liked, and now found myself on the verge of tears.

His eyes went a little wide and he scratched his chin. "Man . . . that *is* bad."

I started crying full on now, and I hugged him, hoping to find some escape from the world inside the warmth of his varsity jacket.

"Babe, relax. It's only a test."

"I'm screwed, though, Brad. Totally screwed."

He said nothing, and in that instant, I hated him (however briefly) for not finding some inspirational words for me—to tell me that it was all going to be okay—to tell me I had nothing to worry about—to tell me that I'd ace the test the next go-around. Yes, I knew the truth was quite different, but sometimes you just want to hear lies.

"Maybe you can tutor me, Brad," I said through my tears, face pressed against his sweatshirt. I hadn't even thought it through, but at the moment it seemed like a good idea. "Maybe you can give me some pointers."

"Uh . . . sure."

I pulled back and wiped my eyes. *Really? Might there be hope in the world?*

"You will?"

"Sure, why not?" he said, and tousled my hair.

I gave him a big kiss.

"What would I do without you? You're the best."

He winked and checked his watch. "Listen, I've got to go see Coach before classes start, but I'll come by tonight and we'll study. Are your parents going to be around?"

"Yeah, but if you're helping me it'll be okay."

"Really?"

"Absolutely."

I wasn't so sure of that—but desperate times called for desperate measures.

Guilford High was like most schools, I suppose, and nowhere was that more evident than in the cafeteria at lunch. It was the usual mix of style sluts and stoners, post-punks and preps, nerds and nobodies, and everything in between. Every group had their table, and the "cool clique," headed by Tori Clemens, was always staked out at the big round table by the window. There, among her countless ass-kissing friends, she'd hold court and compare purses or shoes or jewelry—whatever it was that she and her too-cool friends did to pass the time in their vapid lives.

The Sistas of Luv, on the other hand, held no such pretensions. We liked to think of ourselves as above the whole bitchy clique thing. Life was too short! Back in seventh grade—at Sandra Birnbaum's Bat Mitzvah party at the Guilford Country Club—Jen, Molly, and I had made a solemn oath never to become those obnoxious girls, and to this day we'd held to it. Don't get me wrong—we were happy to put a guy in his place who didn't know how to treat a girl, but as a rule, we didn't take down other girls like Tori and her posse were prone to do. The way we saw it, a girl had enough problems in this day and age without having to worry about one of her own stabbing her in the back.

Anyway . . .

After seeing Brad, I'd managed to forget about the SAT and how my life was potentially coming to an end. My knight in shining armor was going to save me, and I could let my mind focus on other things . . . like our date on Saturday. Come lunchtime, though, the SAT was *the* topic of conversation, and I began to feel that huge lump in my stomach return. My friends were MIA, so I'd ended up sitting alone for a few minutes, next to the Mathletes' table, of all places. I couldn't help but overhear as they talked about their SAT scores, where they were applying early admission, and how excited they were to build robots in college. I won't bore you with all the details, but let's just say that nobody was talking about State.

Thankfully, Jen and Molly soon arrived, and we all air-kissed before Jen plunked a huge file down on the table in between us.

"What's that?" I asked.

Jen held her hands up dramatically. "This is the article that's going to land me a spot in the Medill summer journalism program at Northwestern."

"It's that long?" Molly asked.

"No, stupid. This is just the research." Jen sat down and motioned for us to come close like she was going to tell us a secret. "I think this article might put me on the front page of the *New York Times,* too."

I should say here that in addition to her skills as a reporter, Jen also has an innate skill for exaggeration—the SAT word would be "hyperbole," I suppose. You see, her dad had been a reporter for the *Times,* and he got killed covering the war in Afghanistan. His Humvee rolled over in a ditch, and he was crushed beneath its weight. Needless to say, Jen and her mom went through a really hard time, and ever since then Jen has devoted her life to journalism. I think she was going to do that anyway, but now it was more than a hobby, it was an obsession.

"What's it about?"

"The SAT," she said.

"Snooze-o-rama," Molly exhaled. "If I hear those three letters again today, I'm going to puke."

"Tell me about it," I agreed, looking down at my food.

"Listen up. I believe that there have been several cases of cheating on the SAT the last four years."

"Really?" I asked, trying to remain as casual about it as possible. "How do you mean?"

"I've been comparing students' scores over the last few

years, both here and at Pinewood, and there's definitely something fishy going on," she continued. "Last year, 10 students at Guilford scored under 1800 and then on the second time around, they managed to get above a 2100. That's like, a three-hundred-point improvement. Typically—nationwide—an average student goes up fifty points the second time around. Three hundred points? That's a statistical anomaly."

"Wow," Molly said. "So you think somebody's cheating . . . like there's a Taker?"

Hearing the word made me shiver in my chair.

"No," Jen replied.

"Really?"

She shook her head. "That's just a suburban legend."

Maybe not, I thought to myself. Maybe the text I'd gotten earlier in the day was real. For once, I had more of a scoop than Jen, but I said nothing. I wasn't looking to win a Pulitzer for investigative reporting. I just wanted to get into college.

"Surely some kids get their scores up that much without cheating," Molly offered.

"Maybe, but it's a total crazy long shot."

"Thanks," I said.

Hello? How 'bout some sensitivity here!

"Oh my God, I'm so sorry," Jen stuttered. "Well, of course it can happen, and it totally will for you . . . I know it," and she trailed off, embarrassed. "All I'm saying is that ten students in one school is off the charts. Someone helped them cheat."

"Who?" Molly asked as she looked around the lunchroom for candidates.

"I don't know. But I'm going to keep an eye on our class. Somebody's gonna cheat, and I'll be there to blow the lid off."

Fan-freakin-tastic. My best friend is going to fink me out if I use the Taker.

I played with my food, feigning disinterest. "So how are you going to do that?"

"I can't tell you. Journalist privilege."

And *I* can't tell you how annoying I found her set of ethics, but what could I do?

I shrugged my shoulders like I couldn't care less.

SURVIVING THE SAT: TIP #2

GUIDANCE COUNSELORS

● ●

Guidance counselors fall into three categories, each with their advantages and drawbacks. Careful consideration must go into selecting which type best suits your personality, as ultimately these people guide you through the SAT and your college application process. Said categories are as follows:

THE ENABLER: This mealymouthed counselor perpetually acts as though you can do no wrong. He or she wants to be your best friend. Flunk a test? *Don't worry, sweetie.* Boyfriend dumps you? *Come into my office and we'll talk about it.* Overreaching on what schools you apply to? *Why not, what have you got to lose?* These never-were-moms lull you into a false sense of security about your future and, rather than doing what they're supposed to (i.e. help you get into college), they prefer to coddle you along and play the role of favorite relative.

THE NAYSAYER: Rather than go out on a limb, this guidance counselor derives sick pleasure from telling you all the reasons why you *won't* get into college. You have a 4.0? *Dartmouth could fill its class ten times over with students with perfect grades.* You're captain of the squash team? *Yes, but you're not nationally ranked.* Found a way to cure cancer? *Keep it to yourself. No one likes a bragger.* Lashing out at you because at some point in the past their dreams were ruined like a bad haircut, these people love to burst your bubble. They are best to be avoided.

THE WHAT-YOU-WANT: This counselor doesn't pamper you or try to be your friend; they're simply interested in getting you to the next step. Remarkably, he or she treats every student with respect and plays no favorites, whether you're going to end up at community college or Yale. While they're not going to blow smoke up your butt and lead you down the primrose path, they will, on the other hand, encourage you to make a go for the best school possible. More difficult to find than you may think.

MRS. G. WAS the coolest lady at Guilford HS, and I was fortunate enough to have her as my guidance counselor. She fell into the last category—*The What-You-Want*. She'd been in the Peace Corps for a while, and her office was decorated with a lot of African masks and things. Some of the teachers raised an eyebrow when she occasionally wore a dashiki—it's like an African robe—but I dug it and liked the fact that she had her own soul and didn't try to hide it. I'm not sure how much she was into working at GHS—she once called the principal a "tiny dweeb"—but the students who had her were thankful.

When I arrived at her office, she looked up from her magazine.

"Glad you came by. . . . How'd ya do?"

I lingered by the door. "You don't know?"

"No, actually I do know. But I wanted to hear you say it. It's important for dealing with the situation."

"So you called the Board?" I asked.

She shook her head. "Your mother called me."

My mother called her?! Oh, the righteous anger is never so true as when your parents rat you out to your teacher. For the third time today—I don't usually cry this much, I promise—tears welled up in my eyes before streaming down my cheeks. Mrs. G. got up, shut the door, and then gave me a big hug. After a beat, she handed me a tissue and motioned for me to sit in the student chair.

"Buck up, kid . . . Crying isn't going to get you what you need."

"But what can I do?"

She was thoughtful for a moment before handing me a calendar with several dates on it. "There's a practice exam in two weeks and another real SAT in eight weeks. . . . Hit the books."

"I'm going to," I said, regaining my composure. "Brad's going to help me study."

"Your boyfriend Brad?"

I nodded. She looked away—unimpressed.

"Sure, you could do that," she began, "but if I were

you, I'd go to the tutorial lab and set up some sessions. I've already spoken with the head of the lab about you. Ronald Gross—do you know him?"

Come again?

"Yeah, I know him." I looked at the floor, trying to mask my horror. *Get tutored? By Ronald Gross?* "But the lab's—you know—sort of for people who need help."

Translation: It's for morons.

"Then set up something else with him if you're embarrassed," she answered, having none of my whining. "Ronald is very good. He's your best chance."

Between you and me, the Taker was starting to look pretty good right then.

"All right, I'll do that," I said, and I got up.

"And by the way, you need to know that in light of your scores, Mr. Fellner wants to meet with you and your parents tomorrow afternoon. He wants you to reevaluate your applications."

What did that mean? Reevaluate? Mr. Fellner was the head of the college guidance office—and notorious.

"Okay," I mumbled, "but I'm still applying to Princeton."

"Of course. He just wants to discuss other options with your parents."

I raised my head high, feeling a lifetime of pressure descend on my shoulders. "There is no other option. My dad's family has gone there forever."

And with that I left. She called out to me to see Gross as I walked out the door, but by that point I wasn't listening. I wasn't going to call Gross, and I certainly wasn't going to reevaluate my admissions plan, no matter what Mr. Fellner said.

I had two classes left in the day, but I went for the front doors of the school and headed for Molly's car. She left after seventh period every day, and today . . . I was getting the hell out of there.

When I got home, they were waiting for me.

It seemed that my father had never gone to work. I'm guessing he'd just sat around all day asking God what he'd done to deserve a daughter who couldn't test. He knew I was smart, everybody did, and on tests in school I was fine. But put a bubble sheet in front of me and I can't even fill out my name properly. None of that mattered now, though. My parents were sitting at the kitchen table, like two parole judges waiting for me to explain myself.

"Why are you home early?" my mother asked.

I dropped my backpack with a thud next to Mr. Biggles's water bowl.

"I couldn't take it anymore. How could you call Mrs. G.? How could you call and get my scores?"

Just as I was getting my own head of steam going for Self-Righteous Outrage . . . my mother let a single tear drop from her eye, looking like a little girl who'd lost her doll. If intentional, it was a masterful counter maneuver to what I'd planned. I was struck speechless.

"You shouldn't have run out of here this morning," my father declared.

"I was late!"

With that, Dad rolled his eyes and Mom attempted to gather herself. My plan was now totally in shambles.

"I'm sorry, Carly, but you left me no choice. What are you going to do now?" my mother managed to get out.

"I'm going to Princeton!" I stuttered. "I'm going to take the SAT again, and Brad's going to help me."

My father sat up straight in his chair.

"Brad? No, Brad's not helping you do anything."

Dad hated Brad. I heard him tell Mom that he didn't trust Brad because he was just like Brad when *he* was eighteen, and therefore knew what Brad wanted. Oh my God, fathers are so annoying.

"He scored 2250, Dad!"

Yes, I embellished a bit, but I needed to sell Dad on this plan.

"Really?" he asked.

"Yeah, and he said he's cracked the system and he's going to teach me how to take the test and get me up at least two hundred fifty points."

"I've always liked that boy," my mother chimed in.

That was an understatement. For better or worse, she thought Brad walked on water.

Dad shot her a look and then turned to me. "Well, I'll give it a trial run, but I want to see what Mr. Fellner suggests in our meeting tomorrow afternoon. I'm sure it won't be Brad."

I sparkled a smile and kissed my father on the cheek. "Thanks, Daddy. Brad won't let you down."

He groaned and then gave me a hug. My mom rubbed my back and said everything would work out.

I know I'm hard on them, but sometimes, actually . . . they're okay.

SURVIVING THE SAT: TIP #3

HOW TO STUDY

● ●

1. ALWAYS have an ample amount of caffeine available, preferably Diet Coke or coffee, but NoDoz is acceptable in a pinch. Under no circumstances is Red Bull permitted—extremely fattening.

2. ALWAYS wear comfy clothing. Sure, you won't find this one in most study guides, but my firm belief is that if you're squeezed into your Sevens, it inhibits blood flow to the brain and therefore the ability to absorb information. A pair of Juicy sweatpants and a zip-up top are my personal choice, but obviously I leave it to your own discretion.

3. ALWAYS allow big chunks of time to work. Let's face it, ladies, the first few hours of studying is inevitably all about cleaning your room, doing your old chemistry homework, or sending thank-you notes for last year's birthday gifts that your mother's been nagging you about—in other words, basically doing anything other than what you really *should* be doing.

4. And most important . . . NEVER study with your boyfriend.

As boys weren't allowed in my bedroom—I know, I often wondered what century my parents were living in—and my mother's Oprah book club was meeting in the living room, Brad and I were in the family room for our first study session. Just last year, my father had taken what had been our cozy family room and (much to my mother's horror) completely gutted it. In its place he'd created what he called his "entertainment hub," complete with gigantic HD television set, TiVo, DVD player, Dolby Surround, subtweeter—or whatever it's called—and basically every electronic toy known to man and boy. It was sort of cheesy, but my mother and I agreed that, all things being equal, better a new room than my father having some other kind of midlife crisis, like buying a Lamborghini or leaving us for a

Russian airline hostess. I'm telling you, I've heard some crazy stories. Fortunately, in this mecca of gizmos there was also a big sofa and an oversize coffee table, so when need be, it was a good place to work on projects—in my mom's case, her crafts, or in mine, studying for the SAT.

I was ready to get started on *Operation SAT Ace*. Let's be honest, my life was hanging in the balance, so in addition to my Starbucks grande latte, SAT study guides, and different color pens, I'd also bought a new spiral notebook that I planned to fill with the vast knowledge of the SAT that Brad was going to impart to me.

Knowledge, however, did not appear to be forthcoming.

"Oh, c'mon!" he shouted over the basketball game on ESPN. "Did you see that—it was a foul!"

Not how I imagined this beginning.

As I saw it, my main problem was on the math section. I know I'd done badly on the critical reading, but that was pure nerves; I figured I could overcome that with a little cup of confidence. But when it came to the math problems, so many of them just didn't make any sense; You know, X leaves the train station going 30 miles per hour and Y leaves two hours later going 35 miles per hour— who gets to point B first? I mean, really, who cares?!

Like I'm ever going to use that in real life? I think not!

"Post up, dude!" he yelled. "Post up!"

"Brad, my mother and her friends are right upstairs. They're going to hear you."

"Sorry."

"We're supposed to be studying down here, you know," I sighed, hoping he might get the hint. Clearly he didn't, because all he did was turn down the sound on the TV.

Typical Brad, I said to myself.

Brad lived for three things in life—sports, sports, and sports. Somewhere I knew that *I* fit in, but sometimes just where, exactly, I couldn't say. Not that I'm complaining, mind you. Brad was a total catch. If you could see him, you'd absolutely agree—I promise. Six foot two, muscular without looking like a meathead, and the cutest blue eyes. And to complete the package, along with being totally dreamy—Brad is smart. Not nerdy smart, but smart enough that he doesn't have to work that hard to get grades good enough to assure him a place at one of the top colleges. I mean, everything just comes easily to him. Sure, I'm better at English and writing than he is, but when it comes to math, he is a wiz and I am a dunce.

"Brad, I really need your help," I said, trying to avoid sounding whiny. "Can you shut the game off?"

"Fine," he huffed. He clicked off the TV and slid down to the floor where I sat. "What problem do you need help on?"

"I don't know. Is there like, a type of question you think we should focus on?"

"Judging from your scores, it's not a matter of what you *do* need help on, but if there's anything you *don't*," he joked, cracking himself up.

"Ha-ha," I replied. "I'm glad you're amused by all this."

"Braaaaad, I need your heeeelp," he said, talking slowly and making word signs on his palm like Helen Keller.

I shoved him onto his back. "That's not funny!"

"Braaaaad," he moaned on.

Deciding that ignoring him was the best way to get him to stop, I opened my Kaplan prep book and busied myself with a problem. It was some kind of circumference question, and whether it was because it was too hard, or I was just distracted by being annoyed with Brad, I couldn't make heads or tails of it.

"I'm sorry," he said as he pushed himself up off his back. "You're not retarded, I'm just giving you a hard time." He laughed again.

I said nothing and just stared at the problem in front of me.

"You're stuck on this one, huh?" he asked.

I nodded. He pulled the book in front of him and glanced at it quickly.

"Oh," he said. "It's really straightforward. You calculate for the radius by taking the square root of eighty-one and then multiply that by two and then multiply by pi. It's *B*."

Radius . . . square root . . . pi . . . well, of course. *Why didn't I think of that?*

"Um, but why?" I asked, hoping for a cogent explanation rather than just the answer.

"It just *is*. Don't you get it? It's simple."

Simple for him, maybe—but not for me.

"Let me try another one," I said.

The next problem was a function question. I was drawing a blank on how to solve it, but soldiered on, praying that the right approach would dawn on me. Brad put his arm over my shoulder and kissed my neck.

"I'm trying to work on this problem, Brad."

"Just use the quadratic formula," he threw out, with his mouth still close to my neck.

"Quadratic formula?"

"You know, B squared minus four A . . ."

"I know the formula, but why am I using it?"

This was totally not helping.

"I have a better idea," he said as he ran his hand up the back of my shirt.

"Not now."

"You smell good."

"Oh, yeah?" I asked, mustering all the irritation in my voice that I could. But to be honest, he was a little hard to resist. Like I said, he was really built—even if we hadn't done the deed yet.

"Have I told you lately how beautiful you are?" he said, moving his lips to my cheek.

"I don't think so," I answered, starting to feel a little flush and losing my focus.

"Well, you are."

And as much as I don't like to kiss and tell—a girl's got to have her secrets, right?—a few minutes later we were, well, making out.

"We should keep studying," I breathed, breaking away for a moment.

"Oh, c'mon," he said.

"Well . . ." But he kissed me again and I didn't stop him.

"We'll get back to the SAT in a little bit," he whispered.

I *should* have said no. I *should* have said that we had to study. I *should* have kept us focused on the all-important operation at hand. But as usual I didn't want Brad to get annoyed. He could be . . . well . . . touchy. I've really got to learn that it's okay to stand my ground.

Things were starting to get a little heavy, and just as he began unzipping my warm-up jacket, just about the worst thing ever happened.

"So is this what qualifies as studying these days?" I heard a deep voice say.

I looked up.

Oh my God.

Standing right behind us . . . was my father.

SAT Vocabulary Builder:

bolt

Definition: 1. *v. slang.* to leave a location or situation quickly 2. *n.* a device that secures a door. (Obviously not functioning in this scenario.)

discomfit

Definition: 1. *v.* to make self-conscious, embarrass, mortify or humiliate.

"Did you just die?!" Molly exclaimed on the other end of the line.

"Just about! I've never been so embarrassed in my whole life."

"That's like, an invasion of privacy," Molly concluded as I heard her clicking away on her keyboard in the background, no doubt IM-ing while we were speaking. My luck, she was probably telling Jen what had happened, who would put it in her gossip column. "It's like treading on your constitutional rights."

"Oh, right," I answered.

"I hope you yelled at your dad, though," she continued. "That's ridiculous—I'd never let my parents do that to me. My therapist says it's important to set boundaries with them. I've told you how you need to deal with them, you know."

"Of course I yelled," I replied. "I really let him have it for sneaking up on us."

Truth is, I did nothing of the kind. Molly is the type of girl who will have knock-down-drag-out fights with her parents if she doesn't like something they do. Maybe it's the dramatic actress in her, but she never hesitates to tell them how she feels, whether it is about her curfew, going on a date on a school night, or what her mom is serving for dinner. For some reason, though, I am not capable of doing the same. Sure, I claim to, but the reality is that I usually just roll over to whatever my parents want or insist upon. Let's just say, for instance, that as already evidenced, I was much better at Self-Righteous Outrage in theory than I was in practice. I like to think it was because I am a "good daughter," but I suspect it's because I don't have the nerve to stand up to them. I tell myself that when I get to college it will be different.

If I get into a college, that is. . . .

"So are you going to study with Brad again?"

"Oh, sure. That would go over real well with my parents now," I answered. "Not a chance in the world that they'd let me."

"Mega bummer."

"Totally."

"So what are you going to do?" she asked.

The million dollar question. I had no idea. I was now a day closer to the next SAT test date and still just as far from a decent score. Just as I was starting to ponder faking a life-threatening illness, the other line on my cell phone beeped. I checked the number—RESTRICTED.

"Molly-poo, gotta go. It's Brad. He said he'd call me when he got home."

"That's fine, blow me off," she said. "Kidding. Later, Cars."

I clicked over and started speaking without saying hello.

"How horrible was that? I'm soooo sorry."

There was no response on the other end of the line.

"Brad, are you there?"

"Did you really think Brad was going to be the answer to your problems?" a male voice said.

"Very funny, Brad. Are you home already?"

"This isn't your boyfriend," the man said, more clearly now.

It *wasn't* Brad.

"You must have the wrong number," I said. "I think you made a mistake."

"There's been no mistake."

"Who is this?" I asked. I was starting to feel like someone being stalked in a horror film.

"I'm here to help you," the man answered. "You know who I am."

I thought a beat, and then it hit me.

"You mean . . . are you . . . the Taker?"

"I am."

Holy sh-!

"So you're real?"

There was a long silence. For a moment I thought he had hung up, frustrated by my questions.

"Hello?" I said.

"I'm losing my patience," he said.

"Sorry, hold on." I opened the door to my bedroom to make sure the coast was clear and no one was in the hall listening, before shutting it again. "Are you positive you're not just messing with me? Ralph, is this you?!"

Come to think of it, this was totally something that Molly's brother would do!

More silence. "No, this is *not* Ralph."

"How do I know this isn't—"

He talked over me. "I don't have time for games," he said. "Do you want my assistance or not?"

I thought a second. "Well, um, how does this work, exactly? I mean, is there like, a contract or something?"

"It's straightforward. I take your SAT for you, and I guarantee you a score within one hundred and fifty points of perfect. That's it."

Within a hundred and fifty points of perfect? Wow! Princeton would love that.

"How do you do it? I mean do you go to—"

"That's of no concern to you. All that matters is that, if we are to do this, you will sign up for a course like Kaplan, or Lettich's, or one your school offers. Otherwise it'll look too suspicious when your score goes up. Then, when the day comes for the actual test, you will go to the exam center and take it—just like before—but you'll be quite pleased when you get the results back."

"Riiiight," I said as I turned it over in my mind. It sounded so easy, so perfect, so . . . too good to be true. "So that's it?"

"That's it."

"And like, how much do I have to pay you?"

He said nothing for a few moments. "There's no upfront fee for my services. Instead, after you get your scores back—and they're as good as I say they're going to be—you'll do something I ask. Or I'll expose you."

Do something that I ask? That was vague. I imagined all the possibilities. Ewwww. Actually, it was frightening.

"I can't agree to that," I said. "You'll have to tell me your price now."

"Then we have no deal."

Silence. This was crazy!

"Nice talking to you, Carly. . . ."

"Wait!" I yelled before he had a chance to hang up.

"Let's say for some reason I change my mind. How do I reach you?"

He exhaled. "Send me an e-mail. The address is 'take-forme@hotmail.com,'" he explained. "But don't write anything in the body of the e-mail about the SAT or anything—understand? Just send me 'flowers' from virtualflorist.com, and I'll get in touch with you. That way we leave no traces of what we're doing."

Send a virtual plant? Okaaaay. It seemed kind of ridiculously cloak and dagger, but I guess we were dealing with cheating on the SAT.

"How long do I have to make a—"

But he'd already hung up.

Thinking fast, I hit *69 . . . but the number was blocked.

So the Taker is real.

Please answer the following question on the basis of what was <u>stated</u> or <u>implied</u> in the previous chapter.

It can be reasonably inferred from the passage that the Taker is

    (A) a shady dude

    (B) very smart

    (C) strangely knowledgeable about my life

    (D) a pedophile

    (E) all of the above

AT SCHOOL THE NEXT DAY, I couldn't get the conversation with the Taker out of my mind. Should I have accepted his offer? Wouldn't that have made my life so much easier? Or was I right to trust my instincts and say no? I just couldn't decide.

Let me make one thing clear: this is no cheater's bible. I've never cheated on any test in my life. Never snuck a cram sheet into an exam, never glanced at someone else's paper—nothing. It might sound a little Goody Two-shoes, but it's absolutely true. I'd like to say that it's a moral thing, but I think it's probably more about pride. I prefer to stand on my own two feet.

But this case, of course, was entirely different. This wasn't just one test that would get factored in along with attendance, class participation, and papers for a final grade. The SAT stood alone, and it meant everything for my future. Maybe it would be okay this once to blur the line between right and wrong. Presidents do it all the time, don't they?

After lunch, I swung by the offices of *The Guilfordian* (our newspaper) to see Jen. I wasn't sure how much I wanted to tell her, but I needed some girlfriend advice on this one. When I arrived she was poring over the same huge file from lunch the day before.

"Figured it out yet?" I asked with a laugh.

She smiled and pulled her hair back in a ponytail. "I'm onto something here. Believe me!"

"If you say so," I said. "But when you find out the secret, let me know. I could use the help."

"Trust me," she answered. "The whole school's going to know."

We laughed, and right when I was going to ask her for advice, the faculty adviser for the newspaper, Miss Healy, came in, and Jen went over to talk to her. Alone now with her file in front of me, I tried to read some of the documents—albeit upside down—but it was all a jumble. It did seem that she'd made tons of lists: study courses, teachers, guidance counselors, and students, all apparently cross-referenced, but from where I was standing, I couldn't make sense of it. It all pretty much looked like hieroglyphics. Penmanship was never one of Jen's strong suits.

A moment later she returned.

"So what's up?" She said.

"Can I ask you a question—privately?"

"Totally."

I sat down. "But you can't say anything to anybody."

She nodded.

"Let's say a guy told you that if he did something for you, you had to do whatever he asked for." I took a breath. "What do you think he'd want?"

She folded her hands in her lap. "Well, that's simple. Sex."

My worst fears were confirmed.

"You really think?"

"Or some version thereof," she continued. "You know, the deed itself or maybe going d—"

"Stop, stop, stop! I've heard enough!" I yelled. "You don't think maybe it could be money?"

Jen considered this. "I guess it could be money. But more likely than not, I'd go with sex."

"Got it," I said, feeling dejected and horrified.

After a few moments, her eyes went wide and her voice dropped low. "Is this about Brad pressuring you again to sleep with him? You've got to tell that overgrown boy that you're not—"

"No, no, it's not about Brad," I said—although he *had* been pushing me for months now. I smiled and played with my necklace. "Actually, it's for this new short story I'm working on."

"Oh, sounds cool."

"Sometimes it's hard to get inside a guy's head, you know?"

She smirked. "Tell me about it."

It may be hard to get into a guy's head, but clearly the Taker had gotten himself into mine.

Come three o'clock, my parents and I were sitting in Mr.

Fellner's office discussing my college prospects. Mr. Fellner, known to the student body as Tom "The Terminator" Fellner, had been lured to GHS the year before because, during his tenure at our archrival Pinewood, he'd boasted a ridiculously good track record for getting students into the best colleges. Just how he got "the Terminator" moniker was for different reasons, though, and I think our principal would've liked to have adjusted this part of his latest hire. Mr. Fellner was called "the Terminator" because he was harsh. And not kind of harsh—I'm talking shoot-your-dreams-down-in-flames-and-rip-out-your-heart-before-your-very-eyes harsh. While delivering his withering assessments of their futures, Mr. Fellner had reduced no fewer than eleven students to heaping masses of tears, and rum or had it, Frankie Lin had even thrown up in this very office.

Now it was my turn to get the aforementioned treatment.

"I've spoken with Mrs. G. about your SAT scores," Mr. Fellner began, "and I have to be honest; I think we need to reassess what schools you're applying to."

"Gotcha," I said, waiting to see where this was all going. My father shifted next to me.

Mr. Fellner opened a manila folder on his desk and

handed applications to me and my parents, one by one.

The University of Maryland.

Not too bad, I guess.

North Dakota State University.

Where?

Colchester Community College.

I thought I was going to faint.

"This is ridiculous," I heard my father start to bluster next to me. "A community college?!"

Mr. Fellner shrugged his shoulders. "Everybody needs a safety."

"Absolutely ridiculous," Dad battled back.

The Terminator leaned back in his chair and folded his arms. "What can I say, Mr. Biels. I'm just a realist."

"But this . . ." my mother whimpered, "this is . . ." She couldn't even finish her sentence, and I suppose my father did her a favor when he jumped in.

"Our plan has always been *Princeton* for Carly. She's a legacy there. After all . . ."

I closed my eyes, knowing exactly where he was going.

". . . *I* went to Princeton, my father went to Princeton, and so did my father's father. I'm on the board of the Ivy Club, and I've been very generous with alumni giving over the—"

But now it was Mr. Fellner's turn to cut someone off.

"That's all very nice and well, but with these scores, it will be nearly impossible—alumni or not," he said. "It would be futile."

Everyone went silent.

Now, I admit that my scores weren't very good, but to feel so thwarted by someone who was supposed to be helping you—wasn't that his job? why the school paid him?!—was enough to make me want to spit. In an effort to somehow balance out the karmic wrong I was being done, I started to imagine the pathetic life that this little Napoleon of a man must have. Judging from the wood veneer furniture in his office—his home was right out of Ethan Allen—and his clothing? The pleated Dockers, the thin brown suspenders and the faux-suede Hush Puppies? It was a total 911 to *Queer Eye for the Straight Guy*! And as for his wife (which a ring on his left hand evidenced), I imagined some dowdy, peanut of a woman, who—though mousy, pale, and suffering perpetually from bad breath—was actually the one who wore the pants in the family. Yes, his sad, useless, sorry-excuse for an existence was all becoming one hundred percent clear to me. I began to relax as I realized that, though I may have been unhappy right then, Mr. Fellner would be unhappy for the rest of his life.

Just as I was starting to feel confident of my unflagging superiority, my bulletproof assessment of Mr. Fellner was thrown into question when I spotted a set of car keys on a Porsche key ring sitting on his desk. He drives a Porsche? On a teacher's salary? No way, I told myself. It was probably just wishful thinking on his part. He'd probably bought the key ring at a dealership and—

"Surely there must be something we could do," I heard my mother implore. My father grunted in agreement.

"For Carly to even have a shot at Princeton, she'd have to get her scores up about . . ." He opened my file and scanned through it like a doctor visiting the terminally ill. "She'd have to get them up by about four hundred points."

Four hundred points! Oh, sure! That was just about as likely to happen as me getting Pamela Anderson's chest! (Then again, if she could pay to make it happen, I guess I could, too.)

Mr. Fellner leaned forward. "There is an SAT study class that one of our former teachers runs. David Lettich— do you remember him?"

Mr. Lettich—aka Mr. *Letch*? Um, yuck! The teacher who would always look down your shirt when he passed out exams? The one who you could always catch checking out your butt in the—

"Well, Mr. Lettich has done remarkable work getting students' scores up, but unfortunately, I don't think he has any slots left in his intensive course. I could try to pull some strings, but to be perfectly frank, I'd be reluctant to recommend Carly to him, because there are other students who . . . well . . . show more promise; students for whom it could make a real difference."

My father cleared his throat and set his elbows on the Terminator's desk. From his body language I knew already what was going to happen. Isn't it amazing how we can read our parents sometimes?

"Mr. Fellner. Hear me. If this Mr. Lettich is as good as you say he is, I want my daughter in that class. Are we understanding each other?"

I know it doesn't sound like much, but my father can be pretty damn intimidating when he wants to be. And boy, was he ever. I tingled ever so slightly with excitement. *You go, Dad!*

The Terminator—thrown ever so slightly for the first time in the meeting—removed his glasses and pinched his nose in thought. After a beat, he looked up again.

"I'll tell you what. Week after next, the school is giving a practice SAT. If Carly takes that, and gets her score up by at least a hundred points, I'll recommend her to Mr. Lettich."

I wanted to high-five my dad right then and there, but I remained still. My father nodded to himself before turning to me. "That's fair. She'll get studying right away."

"I should warn you that Mr. Lettich's course is not . . . shall we say . . . inexpensive," the Terminator threw in, as if he wanted to regain the high ground.

"We're talking about my daughter's future here," my dad answered, undaunted. "Money is not an object."

Okay—that part gave me a stomach dropper.

But in that split second, I could have sworn Mr. Fellner's lips curled into the slightest of smirks before he closed my file. "Well, I suggest you get studying, then, young lady."

On the car ride home with my uncharacteristically quiet parents, however, I felt my good spirits start to fade. Yes, my dad had won with Mr. Fellner, but so what? Let's say by some miracle I did get my scores up by a hundred points in two weeks. Let's say I did get into Mr. Lettich's course. I'd still have to get my score up three hundred *more* points. And like Jen said—that would be a crazy long shot. Outside of Mr. Lettich plugging me into a computer that would give me SAT skills like Keanu learns kung-fu in *The Matrix*—it just wasn't going to happen. No, the victory that my father had won for me had been a hollow one. The Terminator was right: as it stood, Princeton was just a pipe dream, and without real help, that's all it ever would be.

For better or worse, I made up my mind.

When I got home, I went right to my room and turned on my computer.

With hands slightly shaking, I logged on to the Internet and went to virtualflorist.com.

And with the press of a button . . . I sent a bouquet of roses to the Taker.

FROM: takeforme@hotmail.com

TO: Carly Biels

DATE: October 18, 01:53 EST

SUBJECT: Your Flowers

C—

As I understand that you now want to move forward with what we discussed, here are the eight rules:

1. Do not stop studying.

2. Sign up for a study course at school or privately.

3. Do not discuss the Taker with anyone.

4. Do not try calling the Taker (btw, I prefer red tulips over roses).

5. You must show up and take the test.

6. You can only use the Taker for one test a year.

7. Once you agree to use the Taker, you cannot change your mind.

8. If you violate any of the rules above, the Taker will expose you as a cheater.

If you accept these terms, I'll meet you at 9:30 Sunday night in Lot A at the mall. Come alone.

—The Taker

P.S. Don't bother replying to this e-mail address. The account will be closed by the time you receive this.

On Friday night, Brad goes to a party where there are 30 single girls, 12 taken girls, and 35 guys. He runs into a girl at the keg at random and she strikes up a conversation with him. What are the odds that the girl he is talking to is single and available?

    (A) 1 in 30

    (B) 1 in 12

    (C) 1 in 77

    (D) 1 in 42

    (E) Far too likely, as far as Carly is concerned

THE NEXT MORNING, I thought about the e-mail I'd received from the Taker. We were to meet at 9:30 P.M. on Sunday night, in the garage of the Crossroads Mall. An empty parking lot—late at night—alone with some older guy who helped people cheat? I'd begun to regret my decision already.

There wasn't much time to rehash it with myself, however, because my parents were harassing me about studying for the practice SAT. The conversation between my mother and Mrs. G. must have been lengthier than either had let on, because, soon after the meeting with the Terminator, my parents were all over me to start studying with—yes, you guessed it—The King of Cool, Ronald Gross. A school tutor was perfect, as far I was concerned. It was the cover the Taker had asked for and it was signed, sealed, and delivered by my counselor with the blessings of my parents. It was the ultimate cover story; the only problem was that it was with Ronald Gross.

Phone calls were traded, e-mails were sent and, come Friday night, instead of getting ready to go to Tori Clemens's party with Brad and the Sistas of Luv—where everyone who was anyone was going to be—I found myself grumbling as I loaded my backpack to go over to Ronald's house to "study." Yes, my life was getting better by the minute. I couldn't tell Jen or Molly that I wasn't going to the party because I had to study with Ronald—it sounded too pathetic—so instead I'd said that my family had relatives in from out of town for the night. It seemed to work. The Sistas offered their condolences.

But you know you're in extra-deep trouble when your parents start cracking jokes about your social life. Isn't that what they call adding insult to injury? When I told my dad I was leaving to go to Ronald's house for my tutoring session, he looked at me sternly, took off his glasses, and said . . .

"Remember, young lady. No cuddling with The Brain."

Yeah, that's my dad's idea of joke. I knew he was still mad at me for hooking up with Brad under his nose, but instead of just coming out and saying it, he made lame jokes. My mom would say it was the Irish in him—but from what I could tell, it was just the dad in him.

Ten minutes later—and now feeling totally depressed that I was about to spend my Friday night with Ronald Gross—I rang the bell to Ronald's house. The door swung open and Mrs. Gross was standing there with a grin from ear to ear.

"Carly! Ronald's been waiting for you," she exclaimed.

Let me point out here that, for every freak, there's a mother freak. Just so you can get a mental image of the being that was now clutching me with rapture—let me describe: Mrs. Gross was wearing a black tube skirt, a white frilly blouse (you know, like the kind guys used to wear with tuxedos in the '70s), and a hot pink cardigan, all of which were wrapped around a barrel-shaped body that could've been a sumo wrestler's.

"Sorry I'm a little late," I said, once I'd freed myself from her grip.

"Not at all, dear. Ronald's just anxious to make your dreams come true."

Dreams? This was going to be worse than I'd imagined.

"Ronald, your guest is here!" Mrs. Gross shouted up the stairs.

While I waited there awkwardly—fearful of what she might say next—I surveyed the house. No voodoo dolls sitting around, or anything. The collection of porcelain cats on the fireplace mantel did make me pause, though.

"Hey, Carly," Ronald said from the top of the steps. He motioned for me to come up.

I scooted by the very round Mrs. Gross and climbed the stairs.

"Shall I make you two some drinks?" his mother called after us. "Maybe some Shirley Temples or virgin daiquiris?"

"No, *Mother*," he said. I took this as a good sign—at

least he recognized his mother's craziness. "We don't need *anything*, thank you."

I followed him down the hallway, past pictures of him in one awkward phase after another, until he turned right in to his bedroom. Unlike most boys' rooms that have posters of athletes and swimsuit models (btw, do guys really think that seeing half-naked girls with ridiculous bodies is going to get *us* in the mood?) Ronald's room was different. On the far wall there was a life-size poster of Albert Einstein, and two entire walls were covered, top to bottom, with bookshelves. I'd never seen so many books in a guy's room in my life. I guess that's what people like Ronald did on weekend nights.

It was when I put my book bag down, though, that I noticed that the far wall was covered with Plexiglas, and someone—Ronald, I suppose—had written a really long math equation on it. It was right out of that movie *Good Will Hunting*. Sadly, Ronald was no Matt Damon, and, between you and me, it kind of freaked me out.

I waved my finger at the wall. "What's all that?"

Ronald turned around to look, and then smiled. "Oh. It's Fermat's theorem."

Fermat's theorem. *Right.*

"It's a math problem from the seventeenth century that

was solved only recently," he explained. "That's part of the answer. I copied it."

He copied math problems down for fun. You see what I was dealing with? Help!

Just then, the ever-meddling Mrs. Gross poked her head in.

"I'll just shut the door to give you kids some privacy."

"No!" I shouted.

Mrs. Gross and Ronald both looked at me like I'd lost it. Okay, maybe I'd shouted a little too loudly.

"I hate closed doors," I covered. "I'm claustrophobic."

Good thinking, Carly. Big words impress this group.

"But it's a big room," Mrs. Gross persisted.

"Mother," Ronald huffed, embarrassed. "Just leave it open."

She pursed her lips and backed out of the room. I noted that she still insisted on closing the door halfway.

"I'm sorry," said Ronald. "She's acting . . . bizarre."

I shrugged my shoulders, giving him the benefit of the doubt. "It's called 'parental-tardation.' All parents suffer from it."

"Parental-tardation," he repeated with a chuckle. "That's funny."

I smiled.

As he thought about the term more, and said it again, he started to laugh. Then he started to laugh and snort. Then he just snorted. He was acting like it was the funniest thing he'd ever heard.

"It's not *that* funny, Ronald."

He stopped snorting and went serious. "Right. I'm just going to run downstairs to get my bag, and then we'll get started."

And he left.

I put my head in my hands. I wanted to cry. What was I doing here?! I should've been out with my friends, like every other warm-blooded teenager on a Friday night. I imagined all the fun everyone was having at Tori's party— the stories people would have, the bits of gossip—and I was going to be totally out of the loop.

Desperate for some connection to the world of the normal, I pulled out my phone to send Molly a text. But just as I did, it started to ring. It was from RESTRICTED. Was it the Taker?

I pressed the green send button on the phone, my thumb twitching.

"Hello?"

"Hey, babe," Brad cooed on the other end of the line. "We're missing you over here, you know."

"I'm so glad you called. Is it just tons of fun?" I asked as my spirits sank even lower.

"It's cool," he said. "The new swimming pool is awesome."

Ronald returned with his bag and waved. I turned away.

"Are people like, swimming?" I asked.

"Yeah," Brad answered. "In their underwear. It's crazy!"

It just had to get better, didn't it? My boyfriend was at a party with girls swimming in their underwear.

"How's it going with your relatives?"

"Oh, fine. We're just sitting down for dinner," I lied. "We've just been talking about their daughter, who's starting kindergarten next year. She's really cute."

Out of the corner of my eye, I saw Ronald shoot me a look.

"Huh," Brad concluded, now bored. I heard a girl yell playfully in the background. "Well, I just wanted to say hey. I'll talk to you tomorrow."

"Will you call me later tonight?" I asked.

He was silent a moment. "Yeah, I'll try. But I might be out late with the guys."

"Okay," I said.

Somebody shouted Brad's name. He yelled back. "I gotta go. Later, sweetie."

"I love you," I called after him.

But he was gone.

I closed the phone and slid it into my pocket. Why did Brad make me feel so lousy sometimes?

"Your boyfriend?" Ronald asked from the bed. "Brad Korian, right?"

I didn't say anything.

"Big party tonight at Tori Clemens's house, huh?"

I turned on my heels.

"Let's just get one thing straight, Ronald. These tutoring sessions that we're doing—they're on the total D.L., got it?"

Ronald looked at me. "D—L?"

He was hopeless.

"The Down Low! Top secret! Goes no further than the two of us!"

He nodded, understanding now. "Oh, sure." He thought a beat. "Well, Mrs. G. knows."

"And that's fine," I said, pulling my hair back. "But no one else. Do we understand each other?"

We were quiet for a minute. For some reason, I just couldn't shake my now-awful mood.

"So what do you want to work on?" Ronald asked.

"I don't know," I said, surely pouting. "I don't really want to do *anything*. I'm only here 'cause Mrs. G. and my parents said I had to, you know. This isn't exactly my fantasy Friday night."

"No," he said to the floor. "I guess it isn't."

Silence again.

"Well, if you're really not into it, then why don't you just do your own thing for the next two hours," he said. "You can study on your own here if you want, and I have my own things to do anyway. I don't want to force anything on you."

"Fine."

At least I won't have to talk to him.

I sat down on the floor and opened my study guide. Crossing to the window, Ronald bent over and looked through a large telescope at the night sky above.

I bet he uses that to look in my window, I said to myself.

But an hour later, after having sat there in silence "studying" (which was actually just me stressing about what was happening at Tori's party), while Ronald read some book called *The Elegant Universe*—a plan hatched in my mind.

Was it risky? Maybe a little. But sometimes you have to be resourceful.

Scanning the page of math problems in front of me, I picked one out where I was certain of the answer. I handed Ronald the book.

"The answer on this one is *D*, right?"

He looked at it briefly, nodded, and smiled. Remarkably, Ronald didn't seem fazed about how bitchy I'd acted before. "Exactly—great," he said. "See, you'll get the hang of this."

"This has been really helpful tonight."

"But we didn't *do* anything, actually," he replied, raising an eyebrow. "You just sat there."

I shrugged my shoulders and ignored his annoying-but-true statement. "Listen, I need a favor, Ronnie," I opened. "I really should go see Brad over at Tori's party."

"Sure, go whenever you want."

"Well, my parents are sort of expecting me to be studying with you until eleven." I gave him my best Oh-won't-you-help-a-poor-defenseless-girl look. "Could you cover for me if they call?"

He thought a beat. "I don't think so, Carly. I don't like to lie."

I resisted stomping my foot. I should've known that Ronald would be a stick-in-the-mud!

"On the other hand," he countered as he stroked his chin, "if we *both* went, strictly speaking then, you are *with* me. And we could just be . . . well . . . studying at a different location."

I smiled, realizing that he was willing to play ball. Perhaps I'd underestimated Ronald Gross. But it all made sense. I wanted to see Brad, and Ronald wanted to go to a party the likes of which he'd surely never get into otherwise. It was a fair trade. Nonetheless, ground rules had to be established.

"Here's how this'll work: I'll get you into Tori's party, but once we're there, we're not there 'together.' You do your thing and I'll do mine. And no mention to anyone that you're tutoring me." I put out my hand for a shake. "Deal?"

Ronald grinned and sat up straight. "You have the com, Mr. Sulu."

"What?"

"Mr. Sulu, you know, from *Star Trek*. When Captain Kirk would give over command to someone else—"

"Ronald," I cut him off.

"Yeah?"

I put my fingers to my lips. "Don't speak."

And off we went.

RONALD KNEW A shortcut across the park to Tori's neighborhood, and it took us under ten minutes to get there. I was less than happy about showing up to a party sans makeup and dressed like a schlump—particularly around the likes of Tori Clemens—but that would be fixed upon arrival.

As we crossed the expansive lawn leading to Tori's front door, I saw Ed "The Thirteen-Year-Old Genius" Rice and two other Guilford nerdy types sitting on the front steps, chin in hands. I assumed (correctly) that they hadn't been allowed in.

"Hey, Ed," Ronald said behind me as I rang the door-bell.

"Hey, Ronald."

There was some shouting and singing from inside Tori's house, but no one answered the door. I rang again.

"You guys coming to the debate team meeting on Tuesday?" I heard Ronald making small talk. There were a bunch of yeses.

After a beat, I glanced over my shoulder and caught Ed and company pointing at me and Ronald, trying to figure out what was going on. Ronald was giving them the thumbs-up.

Great.

Suddenly the door flew open, and Rick Sorenson—who was the type of guy for whom the word "meathead" had been invented—was in front of us, clad in a makeshift toga.

"Carly Biels, what's happening!" And he gave me a boozy hug that lasted a second or so too long. "Come join the party."

"Thanks, Rick."

I walked in, but when Ronald tried to follow, Rick put his hand on Ronald's chest. "Where do you think you're going, Gross Man?"

"Uh," Ronald mumbled, looking like a deer in headlights.

"Let him in, Rick," I said. "He's invited."

Rick made a face like I was crazy. "Whatever."

Ronald nodded thanks and walked in, but when Ed and his pals tried to follow, Rick slammed the door in their faces.

Inside, the party was going full throttle and the living room was jammed with bodies. I pushed my way through a crush of people, trying to find Molly or Jen, until I got to the kitchen, where there was a more than ample supply of alcohol on the countertops. A couple of freshmen were shotgunning beers.

There was a time when I'd loved coming to parties like this, but I wasn't as into it anymore. If you wanted to keep up in the Guilford social scene, of course you had to go to them—plus Brad never wanted to miss a "kegger"—but I'd already reached a point when I could imagine more interesting things to do with a weekend night than watching idiots get drunk and act ridiculous. I had to believe that there were better things out there, and I had high hopes for post-Guilford life.

"They like music loud, huh!" Ronald shouted behind me. I'd totally forgotten he was there.

I spun around and smiled sweetly. "Have fun, Ronnie! There're usually sodas in a cooler out back."

Translation: Get lost.

For a moment he looked a little hurt, but he got the message and nodded before walking away. Okay, I know I was a little mean, but a deal is a deal and I had stuff to handle. Thankfully, I spotted Molly by the staircase and zoomed her way.

"Cars, I didn't think you were going to be able to make it!" she cheered as she gave me a kiss on the cheek.

"The dinner ended earlier than I thought, so I was able to sneak out," I lied.

"Awesome."

I leaned in close. "But I didn't have any time to get fixed up before I left. Can I borrow your bag?"

Molly nodded and pulled her makeup bag from her purse. I gave her a wink, and in five steps I bounded the stairs leading to the second floor, and ducked into a powder room off one of the guest bedrooms that I hoped would be empty. I was in luck. It was.

I knew about the extra bathrooms in Tori's house, because in middle school Tori and I had been best friends, and I'd had many a sleepover in her veritable mansion. The Sistas of Luv, you see, had originally been four: me, Jen, Molly *and* Tori—but come eighth grade, something changed. I don't really want to get into it all, but let's just say that it was right about that time that Tori decided that boyfriends were more important than girlfriends, and she betrayed all of us. Particularly me. Bad blood was created, and though Tori and I had stayed on diplomatic terms—Guilford was too small to blackball anyone—there would always be a palpable tension to our interactions.

Five minutes later—and now looking party ready—I sauntered back down the stairs and gave Molly her bag back.

"Have you seen Brad?"

She grimaced and thumbed toward the backyard. "Last time I saw him, he was out by the pool."

Giving her arm a friendly squeeze, I told Molly that I'd find her later, and I walked through the dining room—in its cheesy pseudo-Asian style—out the sliding doors to the pool area.

It was pretty much like I'd imagined it would be from Brad's description. Although it was a cool night, people were playing around in the swimming pool and lying on chaises on the patio under heat lamps. Some people were indeed swimming in their underwear, but the impromptu nature of the swimming was definitely forced. I noted that almost all of Tori's girlfriends had brought their bathing suits.

I couldn't find Brad at first—he wasn't with the jocks playing Beirut on the Ping-Pong table, nor was he ensconced by the keg, as most of the other guys who weren't swimming were. I rounded the pool, and it was only then that I caught sight of him. He was hanging out in a hammock with a bikini-clad Tori and one of her friends. *Omigod, is that a thong disguised as a bikini?* They weren't doing anything, mind you, just talking and laughing, but something about it set off alarm bells. For starters, no one likes to find their boyfriend flanked by two girls in bikinis, but it's worse when one of them has the initials T.C.; I knew her methods.

"Carly!" Brad shouted out as he saw me approaching. He rolled out of the hammock and came over to give me a big kiss. At least I'd gotten the kind of greeting I deserved. "I'm so glad you're here."

I smiled, but I was still annoyed to have found him reclining with you-know-who.

"Hey, Car-Bear," Tori said, all perky sweet as she arrived at Brad's side. "Car-Bear" had been her nickname for me back in fifth grade—as in the furry stuffed animal—and at the time it had been a term of endearment, but now I knew she was using it as a put-down.

"Thanks so much for having *us*," I said as I took Brad's hand in my own.

"*We* didn't think you were going to make it."

"I see that," I answered.

Tori twinkled her fingers bye-bye and sashayed toward the house.

First I bomb the SAT, and now Tori Clemens is on the prowl for my boyfriend. I didn't need this stress in my life.

But truth was, Tori would always be Tori. On the other hand—perhaps foolishly—I expected more from Brad. I turned to him and struck what I thought was the perfect tone of both irritation and familiarity. "What were you doing?"

"What do you mean?"

"Over there in the hammock."

He put up his hands. "We were talking, that's all."

"Bullshit. Tori was hitting on you."

"You're being ridiculous," he said, taking my face on both sides and planting a kiss on my nose. "There wasn't anything going on. It's just in your head."

"She's a predator."

Brad's good spirits faded a notch, and I saw his expression harden. "Carly, just chill out. Don't be like this."

It was so frustrating! This was how it always was with Brad. If he didn't like something I did, it was a federal case. But if I ever called him out on anything, I was "high maintenance."

I closed my eyes and channeled calm. "How would you feel if I were in a hammock with two guys draped over me?"

He was silent. There was no quick answer to this one.

Brad stepped forward and gave me a hug. "All right. I get it. Let's just drop it, okay? I'll call you tomorrow and everything will be fine," he said, trying to placate me.

"You're leaving?"

"Yeah. A couple of the guys and I are going to this all-night paintball place. It's really cool." I looked down, dejected. "You said you weren't coming to the party, so I made plans."

"I know."

Brad gave me a quick peck. "Call you tomorrow?"

I nodded, and he left. I knew a lot of girls at Guilford would've given almost anything to date Brad, but I'd have given anything at the moment to just have a guy who cared about me more. Who treated me better.

I caught myself and repeated what Brad had said in my mind. *Nothing was going on. It was all in my head.* Maybe he was right.

After a moment, I glanced over toward the hammock, but instead of Brad and the two girls, there was just a boy—alone—lying on his back, staring up at the sky. It was

Ronald. But if you think he was the very portrait of the rejected loser sitting lonesome in the corner with no one to talk to, you'd be wrong. Actually, Ronald didn't appear to care about any of the high jinks that were going on at the party; not the guys swilling beer at the keg nor the girls in their underwear splashing around in the swimming pool. He was quite content . . . studying the stars, it seemed. And then it hit me. Ronald hadn't really been interested in coming to Tori's party at all. He thought all of this was ridiculous (and it was). The real reason he'd come, was for me.

SAT Vocabulary Builder:

nefarious
Definition: *adj.* flagrantly wicked or sinful

malefactor
Definition: *n.* one who does evil or ill

AFTER MY TOTALLY lame Friday night, I spent the rest of the weekend going from feeling bad about how I'd been mean to Ronald, to worrying about what was going to happen when I had my meeting with the Taker. Sure, I'd had some distractions on Saturday—Brad finally called and, true to form, bailed on our plans for that night . . .

something about having to "hang with the guys"—but for the most part I was filled with a vague feeling of dread about Sunday. And it only got worse the closer it came.

Sunday night, I put on the dowdiest clothes I could find. I didn't want the Taker to get any ideas about my being cute or anything. I took an awful dress from my mother's closet (it made me look thirty pounds heavier) and put on my old owl-frame glasses from the seventh grade (we've all made fashion mistakes). I looked bad—and that was good. Right before I left, I ran back into my room and dug out the pepper spray that Grandma had given me the first time I went to New York.

You're probably wondering how I escaped the 'rents so late on a Sunday night. Well, it was easier than expected. Mom was at her knitting circle, and when Dad asked me where I was going at 9:30 P.M. on a school night, I simply said what any girl my age says when they need an excuse:

"I'm out of tampons."

He shuffled some papers, cleared his throat, and retreated to the living room. Period, tampon, that time of the month . . . any of these words can slay a dad in a matter of seconds. Ladies, I hope you're taking notes.

So out I was, but as I drove Dad's car to the mall, I wasn't so sure I wanted to be out. Who was this creep, anyway? His instructions were bizarre. I mean, the virtual flowers via e-mail was weird enough, but now a rendezvous in the garage underneath the mall? I looked at my cell, and the text said to go to level six (The Very Bottom!!) and to park the car in spot 698. The mall was ten minutes from my house, and it closed at nine o'clock, so I knew the lot would be empty except for some lingering employees who stayed on to slug a few beers at the Applebee's bar. But they'd be parked on the first level.

I pulled into the lot and turned my headlights off, as per the Taker's request, and spiraled down until I got to the sixth basement. It wasn't too dark, except in the far west corner, where a light had been broken. I drove slowly, looking at every number, 78, 79 . . . until I reached the nineties, and with each space from there on, it got darker and darker.

I pulled into 698, trunk first, as requested. I stayed in the car and rolled down the window. Was I insane? Just to score well on a test, I was putting myself in a secluded parking lot, in a dark corner, and rolling down the window to meet with some older guy from who-knows-where. This had "bad call" written all over it.

Above me I could hear voices and tires screeching.

Deciding that I should tell someone where I was—in case I got kidnapped, or worse—I took out my cell and punched up Molly. But what was I thinking? There was no reception all the way down here. I was cut off from everyone. I was totally alone.

When I looked up from the phone, I saw it. Or maybe I heard it. It was a match lighting and then the soft red glow of a cigarette that signaled me from the darkest shadow between the corner and a giant pillar supporting the deck above.

He was there.

I got out of the car and closed the door behind me. As I walked toward him, somehow I was no longer frightened. I knew he was my destiny. My future. That everything I had dreamed of—that everything my parents had dreamed of—was now about to be in the Taker's hands.

I took a deep breath.

"Stop right there," the Taker said. His voice was unnaturally deep.

I froze in my tracks. I was still a good thirty feet away from him, and with the Taker standing deep in the shadows, I could make out only the bare outline of his figure.

"It's better that you never see my face," he continued, after taking a drag on his cigarette. "It's . . . cleaner that way."

I exhaled. I took this as a good sign. If I wasn't going to get close enough to see his face, then surely he wouldn't try anything weird or creepy, right? I guess we were just going to talk.

I waited there for a few beats while he said nothing. From where I was standing, I noted that the Taker wasn't a big man, but he wasn't tiny, either. Sort of an average build, it seemed, and he wore what appeared to be a trench coat—though I suppose it could have just as easily been a poncho. Like I said, I could only make out the vague shape of his body in the darkness.

"Do we have a deal?" he asked.

"Um . . . yeah. I mean, yes," I managed to get out.

"All right," he replied, and I saw the red ember of the cigarette drop to the cement floor. He stepped on it. "You understand my conditions?"

I nodded.

"Listen to me," he said. "*You must keep studying.* Teachers aren't stupid. If you don't crack a book during the next seven weeks and then suddenly your scores go up three hundred and fifty points, it's going to cause some major alarms to go off in people's heads. Got it?"

I nodded. "I'm studying with a school tutor."

"They can tell when students are just phoning it in. I know. So make a real effort."

What did he mean by "I know"? Was he a teacher or something?

"Agreed?" he asked.

I nodded again.

"Don't just nod," he demanded. "Say 'Yes.'"

"Yes," I said.

"Sir!"

"Yes . . . sir."

Can you say 'wack-job'? Then again, this was more along the lines of what I'd expected.

"There is no turning back. There will be no further correspondence between us after this meeting—so consider your decision very carefully."

Hadn't I already made up my mind by coming here? I took a beat, as if I was considering it one last time, but truth was, I was in no condition to reflect on anything. By now, I just wanted to get out of there.

"I want to do it," I said.

"Now remember—when we're through—I'll want something from you."

I looked away and swallowed hard. "I know—but it can't be sex."

In the darkness, I saw him nod. But what did that nod mean? Was he agreeing with me, as in, "Yes, it *won't* be sex," or was he disagreeing, as in, "Yes, it *can* be sex"?

Upstairs, I heard what sounded like a group of guys laughing and then the crack of breaking bottles. The Taker must have noticed the sound as well, because he picked up the pace.

"Then we're finished here," he said.

"Okay," I said, too scared by this point to bring up the sex thing again. Just as I was turning to go back to my car, he called out.

"But there's one more thing." I waited. "I'll need collateral for my services."

Like what? I wondered to myself.

"I don't really have anything with me," I said, in an effort to get out of this final requirement.

"Your bracelet will do."

I looked down at my wrist. Oh, no! The charm bracelet that Brad gave me for our one-year anniversary?! I couldn't give him that. What would Brad say when he noticed it was gone? My mind raced for something else to give the Taker.

"How 'bout I give you . . . my coat?" I threw out. "It's from Banana Republic, and it must've cost—"

"Your bracelet," the Taker repeated. And, as if to slam the door on any other negotiating, he directed further. "Put it on the ground in front of you and then go back to your car and *leave*. Or I will."

What choice did I have?

I undid the clasp—gave the silver chain a little kiss—and laid it on the cold concrete floor. It felt like I was giving away my baby.

As I walked back to the car, I heard no sound of the Taker making any move to go pick it up, and when I pulled away, it still sat there, shimmering on the ground.

People who cheat on standardized tests like the SAT are generally thought of as _____.

    (A) pathetic

    (B) incredibly wise

    (C) possible presidential candidates

    (D) out of their minds

    (E) off of Santa's list

YOU MIGHT IMAGINE that my life became one big party after I hired the Taker—there was no sweating the SAT anymore, right?—but it was anything but. While the fear of being branded *Carly the Failure* was gone, in its place was a much more potent, nagging sense of who I'd become:

Carly the Cheater.

As I stood waiting for Molly to pick me up the morning after my meeting with the Taker, I just couldn't shake loose of the feeling that I'd started down a very dark road. Maybe it was the writer in me, but I began to picture the course my life would take. And it wasn't pretty. Had my bombing the SAT been a prologue to an even nastier tale? A story that would end much later, when local television reporters would interview my neighbors—neighbors like Mrs. Gross—who would look into the camera with an expression of both bewilderment and betrayal before declaring, "I'm shocked. Carly always seemed like such a nice girl." Sure, I was no Hannibal Lecter, but still.

For better or worse, Ronald wasn't outside that morning—he never was on Mondays; why exactly, I wasn't so sure, although I vaguely remembered him saying one time that he taught early tutorial lab or something—so I had plenty of time to catalog all the reasons why I now officially sucked. Needless to say, I was relieved when I heard the whine of Molly's Mustang approaching.

"What up, girl!" Molly shouted over the Patsy Cline song that was blasting from her speakers. Like I said, Molly was old school.

I put on my best happy face and hopped into the car.

As Molly started to tell me about the open audition—

she called it a "cattle call"—that she had gone in on for a new off-off-Broadway show over the weekend, I felt my thoughts of the Taker begin to fall away. The normal goings-on of life—like which lipstick Molly wore—swept in, and it appeared, for a time, that all would be like it had been. Maybe it would be possible to go on with my life as if nothing were different—as if I were still the same old Carly.

"P.S.," Molly said with a small frown as we stopped at the traffic light on State Street. "I called you last night to tell you about the audition, but your dad said you went out? He was really acting weird."

"I just had to get out of the house," I lied. "My parents have been driving me crazy with the whole SAT thing."

Molly nodded and put a comforting hand on my shoulder. "It's all going to be fine. You'll see."

I hoped that what she said would turn out to be true, but I wasn't so sure.

Along with feeling super guilty about lying to my friends—although we all know girls who lie all the time, I was never one of them—I noticed when I got to school that I was feeling something else as well. Something worse. *Paranoid.*

Like some high-school version of Raskolnikov—he's the dude in Dostoyevsky's *Crime and Punishment*, in case you haven't read it—I began to fear that everyone at Guilford knew what I had done. That they knew I was working with the Taker. Striding past people on my way to class, I'd read even the blankest of expressions as knowing accusations, and I wouldn't have been surprised one bit if the PA system snapped on, and I was publicly exposed.

Worst of all, however, was that people who I'd normally be happy to see, started to make me incredibly nervous.

Case in point was Mrs. G.

I was running to the cafeteria to grab a bite before AP chem, when she flagged me down in the hallway by her office.

"Carly!"

I felt my grip on my book bag tighten as my nerves set in. I stopped.

"Hey, Mrs. G.," I said.

"How are you, Carly?"

"Oh, you know," I replied.

She fixed me with a look.

"I heard about the other night."

What?! Less than twenty-four hours into hiring the Taker and I was busted?!

I blinked for a few moments, at a loss for any defense. Do I make an outright denial or should I just confess and hope for clemency? Unable to decide, I switched into spin mode.

"Mrs. G., I can totally explain what happened. You see, I was so worried about—"

"Ronald's time is valuable," she declared, cutting me off.

Hunh? Ronald?

"And for you to not take advantage of his being willing to tutor you—during his free time, no less," she continued, "it's incredibly foolish."

So this was about *Ronald?* About what happened on *Friday* night? I almost began to laugh out of joy—and relief.

"This isn't a joke, Carly. It's your life," she pushed. I guess I smiled. Obviously I hadn't meant to.

"I know. I'm sorry," I answered. "Friday wasn't my . . . you know . . . finest hour."

"Clearly."

"I was upset. About something that had nothing to do with Ronald."

Translation: Brad pissed me off.

But I hoped Mrs. G. could read between the lines so I wouldn't have to spell it out. I spotted a few members of Tori Clemens's posse standing not too far away.

"About a boy, I suppose?"

Thank you. I nodded without looking at her.

"Always remember one thing in life, Carly," she offered. "Never let a boy get in the way of your future."

"You're right," I said. But I couldn't look her in the eyes, so I stared at the linoleum.

"I mean it."

I looked up at her. "I know, Mrs. G. It won't happen again."

She gave me a wink, and that was it. Mrs. G. was cool like that.

"I hope you're going to give it another try with Ronald," she pressed.

"I am. I'm gonna swing by the tutoring lab later."

It was true. I needed to apologize for how I'd acted—even if good ol' Ronnie had ratted me out. More important, the Taker's words about studying were still fresh in my mind.

Mrs. G. nodded before fixing me with a look. "Don't squander this opportunity, Carly."

I stood up straight. "I won't. I'm going to study really hard."

* * *

"You're getting tutored by Ronald Gross?" Jen asked. "Wow."

We were sitting in the offices of *The Guilfordian*. On Mondays I had a period to kill before calc, and although I probably should've been getting a jump on my homework for the night, I usually ended up hanging out in Jen's office and dishing about the weekend. And that's exactly what we were doing. Minus, of course, what I'd been up to Sunday night.

"Yeah, Mrs. G. organized it," I explained. "Ronald's a little strange, but you know . . . I need the help."

While I'd initially resisted copping to the fact that I was studying with Ronald, in the grand scheme of what I was now up to, I thought it was best to lay a few of the smaller things out on the table. Besides, just in case Jen's sleuthing on the SAT cheating ring led her anywhere in my direction, I hoped that the Ronald tutoring thing would throw her off my scent.

Oh, what a tangled web we weave. (That's what Mrs. G. would call a hackneyed piece of writing.)

"I actually like Ronald Gross," Jen said, turning her attention back to her computer. She was working on the front-page layout for the next issue. It seemed the lead article had to do with prescription drug abuse by students. Jen tended to gravitate toward the hard news subjects. "Not *like* like—I don't have the hots for him or anything—but I respect him," she continued. "He's his own person."

That was Jen for you in a nutshell. No nonsense.

"Too bad about the bus, though," she cracked after a beat.

I grinned.

"Do you know that one in ten students in Connecticut has tried snorting Ritalin?" Jen said, taking the conversation in another direction.

"Is that true? Like, for fun?"

"That's what I'm not sure about," she replied, rubbing her neck. "There's a theory that some kids do it so they can study longer—or to get an edge on the SAT."

Ah-ha. So that was how she'd gotten on this tangent.

Before I could inquire about just how snorting Ritalin helped you on standardized tests, I felt a lacrosse stick tap me first on my right shoulder and then on my left.

"I dub thee, Lady Carly," I heard Brad say before he leaned over me. We smooched.

"Hey, Jen," he said.

"Hey," she chirped back without looking up from the computer.

Strange. Jen wasn't usually so icy to Brad.

I swiveled around to face Brad, and discovered that Rick Sorenson was with him as well. Brad and Rick had been buddies for as long as I'd known Brad. They were on the lacrosse team together—shock of shocks—but if Brad was the proverbial golden boy, Rick was the obnoxious, bullying sidekick. He had a habit of always scowling—like he'd watched one too many Rambo films—and I guess he thought that, by never smiling, he looked macho or tough. I never really understood why Brad hung out with him, considering what a dick he was, but I've never been one to pretend to understand male bonds.

And it wasn't like Rick had any reason to be so mean. His father owned some crazy-successful construction business, and they lived in a huge house on Fence Rock. Even better for him was that just this year his parents had bought him a brand new BMW X3. He wasn't exactly a hardship case. But, to give all sides of the story, Brad *had* mentioned one time that Rick's dad put a lot of pressure on him— before getting into building houses he'd been an Olympic pentathelete—and his father had hoped that Rick would be a professional athlete. And given that no colleges were recruiting Rick for sports, it seemed highly unlikely. Whatever the rationale was for Rick's behavior, one thing was certain: he was highly feared by the less-than-athletically-inclined at Guilford.

"Hi, Rick," I said.

Rick lifted his head in the slightest of nods in his typical tough-guy greeting. "Tori's party was rockin', huh?"

I nodded with disinterest. Rick moved across the room and glanced at some files on a nearby desk.

"So what are you guys talking about?" Brad questioned. Usually he couldn't care less about girl talk.

"Oh, you know. Girl stuff," I answered.

"Girl stuff, eh," he said as he started bouncing a lacrosse ball off the floor and catching it in the basket on his stick. Out of the corner of my eye I saw Jen look up at him, annoyed. "We're playing Palmer on Thursday—you coming?"

"Big game," Rick seconded.

Out of courtesy to Jen, I grabbed the lacrosse ball midbounce. "I'd love to, but I can't. I have to study for the SAT."

"Can't you study after the game?" Brad pushed.

I didn't want to say that I hoped to have an appointment with Ronald. I'm not sure why I didn't just tell Brad about Ronald, but I suppose it was because I was feeling competitive with Brad—and embarrassed.

I winced and scrunched up my nose. "I'm sorry."

Brad shrugged his shoulders. I tossed the ball back to him.

"You okay, sweetie? You seem a little . . . tense."

"Just focused on the game—that's all," he replied.

"I wish I could be there."

"That's cool—no worries," he said. "Just thought I'd say hey. Talk to you later?"

I blew him a kiss, and Brad and Rick rumbled out.

When the door shut, I leaned in toward Jen. "Brad doesn't know . . . about the Ronald thing."

Jen raised a playful eyebrow. "I gathered."

We laughed.

After a beat, she relaxed back in her chair and spun a pen between her fingers. It was a gesture Jen tended to do when she was thinking about something.

"What?"

"Rick Sorenson," she said, still deep in thought. "I should put him on *the board* as well."

I looked up. "Board? What's 'the board'?"

Jen glanced around the empty office before smiling.

"Come with me."

J EN LED ME into a windowless room in the back of *The Guilfordian* offices that I'd never been in before. From the look of it, the school used it for storage, because, along with dusty boxes full of old issues of the newspaper, there were also stacks of air conditioners and a few rolling blackboards pushed up against the walls. Actually, it would've made a perfect make-out place.

Maybe Brad and I could come here sometime. . . .

"Now, you can't tell anyone about what I'm about to show you," Jen said, ultra-serious. "I don't want the cheaters to know how extensive my investigation is."

Obviously I don't have to tell you what went through my head. I nodded.

"This is *the board*," she announced, and in a swift

motion, she moved to one of the blackboards and flipped it around, revealing the other side.

I stepped back, surprised.

This is really bad.

It was right out of one of those detective shows on TV. The whole board was covered in photographs, charts, and articles, with arrows connecting them. All of it related to her investigation. I nudged closer and saw that there were lists of SAT study groups, classes, tutors, students who'd graduated in the past, students who'd done well on the SAT, students who'd done poorly . . . it went on and on. In the very middle of the board, a series of arrows all led to a circle that had a blacked-out face in it. Beneath the face she'd written *THE TAKER.*

"I thought you said the Taker was a myth?"

"It *is* a myth," Jen answered. "But I had to call the ringleader something on the board, so rather than Mr. or Ms. X, or whatever, the Taker just sounded better. It's really just a placeholder."

Needless to say, I knew different.

"Jen, this is—wow," I breathed, still trying to take it all in—and mask my terror.

What if Jen exposed me?!

"I told you I've been doing a lot of research," she said

with a hint of pride. "Unfortunately, I haven't quite cracked it yet, but at least it's all here. It's just a matter of seeing how the pieces fit together."

So far I didn't see my name anywhere on the board, but I hadn't even begun to study it all. A couple of names did jump out: Ed Price, David Lettich, Tori Clemens, but it didn't look like any of it added up to much yet. And much as I was dying to have an hour at "the board" to see if I could figure out who my Taker was—and make sure there were no links to me—I didn't want to seem like I was too interested. Wouldn't that have just made her suspicious?

"What's this part here?" I asked, unable to suppress all my questions. It was a section with a bunch of newspaper clippings.

"Those are all articles about recent cheating rings that have gotten exposed around the state." She crossed to the board and pulled one of the clippings down.

"This one's funny, actually. In this story, a kid actually did worse on the SAT the second time around, because he hired someone to take the test for him, but the person didn't show up."

Didn't show up? I had to add that to my list of worries with the Taker?

"The kid got caught anyway." Jen said with a laugh.

She took down another clipping. "This one is from this past summer. In this case, a group of kids arranged their seating at the test in a certain way so they could trade answers. One of them was a ringer in math, one was a ringer on the verbal part, and they all worked together."

Pretty smart.

"What happened?"

"They got nailed. Not during the test, but after. The College Board got suspicious when they all got the same answers wrong."

Pretty dumb.

"It was kind of loony, because they were good students, too. It wasn't like they were idiots or anything. They just got greedy and wanted even higher scores. And that's usually when a lot of people get caught."

By now my stomach was churning like crazy.

"So after they got busted, what? They had to retake the SAT?"

She shook her head. "It's not that simple. They're screwed for life. For starters they got expelled from their high school. Worse, the College Board won't let them retake the test now for five years, so they can't get in to any decent colleges. They're probably flipping burgers somewhere."

Would *my* life be reduced to "would you like fries with that"?

"That's the way it goes," I said.

"Yup."

From the hallway, we heard the class bell ring.

"I gotta go," Jen said. I did, too.

We left the room, and just as I was beginning to think that I'd come back when Jen wasn't there to check out the board further, I saw her lock the door with a key.

"Keep me posted on what you figure out," I said as I picked up my backpack.

"Would you actually be up for helping me a little on this at some point?" Jen asked. "There's so much to cover and I can't do it all myself. I need someone I can trust."

Trust. It was like a dagger in my heart.

"Totally. But I'm not sure what use I'll be."

She smiled. "You'll be just what I need."

Which of the following statements about cheating on the SAT is <u>not</u> supported by the previous passage?

    (A) It's very hard to cheat.

    (B) Carly isn't the first person to try cheating on the SAT.

    (C) It takes more than one person to do it successfully.

    (D) If you get caught, you could always go work at McDonald's.

    (E) There is no Taker.

CLASSICAL MUSIC BOOMED from behind the door to the tutorial lab.

I knocked on the door, but instead of an answer, there was just the crescendoing of some symphony or concerto or something. I never listened to much classical music—Mozart sounded just the same as Beethoven to me—so I couldn't tell you what it was, exactly, but whatever was playing, it was big. It was a lot like the music in some lame war movie that Brad made me watch one time.

It was nearly 3 P.M., but I was determined to find Ronald before the end of the day. I tried knocking again—this time harder—but the person inside apparently couldn't hear anything over the music. I turned the knob on the door and found that it was open.

The music was even louder inside. As I entered the offices, I spotted Ronald, alone, with his back to the door. He was flailing his arms spastically—I'm pretty sure he was imagining himself conducting the orchestra—and at different parts of the music, he'd make different gestures, as if summoning more or less sound from different performers. He was caught up in the music, and with his eyes squeezed shut, he turned in my direction and I was able to see his face. He looked like one of those famous conductors you see on the cover of classical music CDs—slightly pained expression, small beads of sweat on his brow, hair askew, but minus the tux, of course. And I know it sounds a little strange, but at that moment, between you and me, he actually looked kind of . . . cute.

I called out to him. "Ronald!"

He didn't hear me.

"Ronald!!"

His eyes popped open and he must've jumped back about ten feet in shock.

"Sorry!" I shouted.

"Hey!" he yelled back over the music and waved. He was obviously embarrassed, and I regretted interrupting him. He ran over to the stereo and turned it off.

"I didn't mean to sneak up on you," I explained, now in the quiet of the room. "But I knocked a bunch of times."

"It's cool, it's cool," he answered not-so-coolly as he tucked his shirt back in.

"What was that you were listening to?"

"Oh, nothing special."

"No, really, I'm curious. Do you listen to a lot of classical music?"

He organized some papers on the desk in front of him nervously. "Yeah, some. It's good to study to, I find. That was Wagner. The *Ring Cycle*."

He smiled, still a bit embarrassed.

"So what's up?"

I took a deep breath. "Listen, I wanted to apologize for the other night. For being kind of bitchy."

He shook his head. "Don't worry about it."

"No, it wasn't right," I said. "I was just . . . wound up about other things. I shouldn't have dragged you to that party."

"I've been to worse," he answered with a shrug of his shoulders. I couldn't tell if he was trying to make a joke or if he was being serious. I pressed on.

"So can we study again tomorrow? And then on Wednesday and Thursday also? I have a time crunch with the practice SAT coming up and . . ."

"I can't," he answered, shaking his head. "I have a Junior League thing with my mother tomorrow."

"Junior League?" I asked, confused. "Isn't that for like, mothers and *daughters*?"

"Don't ask," he moaned. "As you've already seen, my mother is . . . unique."

I made a gesture like I was zipping my mouth shut.

"But I can do Wednesday," he offered.

"Wednesday it is."

"But no parties," he said with a grin.

I winked. "I promise. No parties."

We said our see-you-rounds, but when I got to the door, I still felt like I hadn't entirely made up for my behavior over the weekend.

"Hey, Ronnie," I called out. He looked over to my direction. "You need a ride home?"

His face lit up like a big bright neon sign.

Come 3:15, the parking lot at Guilford was always a mob scene of underclassmen jumping on buses, upperclassmen jockeying their cars to the exits, and fifteen or so desperate outcasts being picked up by their parents. Ronald and I darted between honking cars and shell-shocked freshmen until we found Molly at her parking space. She already had the top down on her Mustang and was reclining in the backseat with a handkerchief tied around her hair. Anyone else attempting this look would've looked like an Eastern European grandma, but on Molly it was glamorous. She called it her Grace Kelly homage.

"I'm ready for my close-up, Mr. DeMille," she said as Ronald and I arrived at her car.

"I told Ronnie that we'd give him a ride home—is that cool?"

"Totally," Molly answered. She climbed into the driver's seat and let Ronald in the back. I took shotgun, and we pulled away.

When we turned onto Union Street and picked up speed, Ronald leaned forward and put his head next to mine on the side away from Molly. "Can I ask you one favor?" he whispered.

"Sure."

"Could you not call me Ronnie? I know people used to call me that, but I'm trying to, you know, rehabilitate my image—and I think Ronald sounds more mature. More masculine."

I smiled. "Of course, *Ronald*."

"If you want to go all out, you could call me Ron, but for some reason, most people don't seem to be going for that."

"Yeah." I laughed. "Let's just go with Ronald."

"That's great. That's great," he said, leaning back.

"So what's going on in your world, big guy?" Molly asked, glancing in the rearview mirror at Ronald.

"Oh, the usual," he sighed, like he rode around with me and Molly all the time. "Getting ready for a couple SAT Twos, doing the tutorial lab thing and, you know, just trying to make the most out of senior year."

"Sounds good," Molly continued. "And what's happening with colleges? You applying early anywhere?"

"I haven't decided yet. Fellner's pushing me to apply to MIT, but I think that's because he has me pegged as a science geek. . . ."

In front, Molly and I exchanged amused glances.

". . . But I want to go somewhere more dynamic, because, frankly, I've seen the girls at MIT. And it ain't pretty."

Oh, Ronald.

"What about now?" Molly asked, treading into waters that—out of kindness—I certainly would've avoided. "You have a lucky lady in your life at the moment?"

"Nah. Why break a perfect streak," he cracked.

I couldn't help but laugh. It was endearing that he had a sense of humor about his situation.

"You're cute, Ronald. You could find a girl," Molly said. "Don't you think, Carly?"

What was it my grandmother said? Oh, yeah: *Every pot has its lid.*

"Um. Sure."

"Kind words," Ronald said. "Very kind."

We stopped at a red light and Molly swiveled around to face him. "It's true. But I'm going to give you some tough love here. You gotta do something about your clothes. Take your shirt for example . . ." And she pointed at his black-and-white M. C. Escher T-shirt—you know those shirts, the ones with the weird drawings where you can't tell the perspective. ". . . Two words: Garbage. Can."

"Really?" he asked.

"Yeah. I'm not being a bitch here, either. I'm just trying to give you some helpful advice."

"I hear ya," he answered.

"And your pleated khakis? Na-uh. I personally would go with cargo pants, but if you're into the chino thing— and hey, that's your prerogative—at least get flat fronts."

"Flat fronts. Right. Anything else?"

I wouldn't have been surprised if he'd whipped out a pad and started taking notes. But Molly has that effect on people. She's cool like that. For starters, she has a terrific fashion sense, but more important—particularly in this situation—she also has a disarming quality, so that even when she's critiquing you, you felt like it was coming from a good place—not a mean one.

"The Docksiders?" I chimed in, now turning around as well. "You planning on going boating sometime soon?"

"Totally!" Molly seconded.

"Got it. Lose the Docksiders."

"You need to send the right signals," I explained. "Girls like to see that a guy knows how to put himself together. They have fashion magazines for guys, don't they?"

"*GQ*," Molly added.

"Exactly. Pick up a copy. It'll give you some ideas."

Ronald was wide-eyed, obviously trying to make sure that he didn't forget any of these pearls of wisdom, and he kept nodding. The car behind us beeped as the light turned green, and Molly started driving again.

"Anything else?"

"We'll send you a bill." Molly giggled and jacked up the radio.

Later, after we'd dropped off Ronald, Molly and I studied each other, both thinking the same thing.

"Were we too harsh with him?" she asked.

"It depends how you define 'harsh.'"

Molly winced—but laughed a moment later. "Years from now, he's going to thank us for that conversation."

And something told me that was true.

THE GROSS METHOD

Copyright Ronald Gross 2005
Handout #1:
General Tips for Taking the SAT.

● ●

1. The questions on the math section are arranged in order from easiest to hardest. Avoid problems that are too difficult for your abilities. Even Superman knew to stay away from kryptonite!

2. Pace, pace, pace. While you want to get the easy questions correct, if you can't solve one, after a limited amount of time, move on.

3. Be clear on what the question is asking you to answer. Many a great mathematician has wasted years with his artillery pointed in the wrong direction.

4. If you can eliminate one of the multiple choice answers, make an educated guess. Since you only lose a quarter point if you get one wrong, the odds are in your favor. If only poker were so easy, I'd be rich!

5. Don't forget to bring a calculator. Would Leonard Bernstein have conducted without a baton?

6. And finally, BELIEVE IN YOURSELF. You have the world's most powerful computer . . . in your head.

QUOTE OF THE DAY:
"Genius is one percent inspiration
and ninety-nine percent perspiration."
—Albert Einstein

MY STUDY SESSION with Ronald on Wednesday was a total trip. For better or worse, I'd entered the Realm of Ronald. As if on a quest for the Holy Grail—which in this case was four hundred more points on my SAT—I discovered that Ronald had a passion for tutoring. Since there were only ten days until the school's practice SAT (and I sure wasn't going to study with him *every* night!), he told me he was doing the greatest hits of "the Gross Method," and that later we'd go back and do more in-depth work. But much as I'd cringed in the beginning about studying with Ronald, it wasn't actually that bad. Sure I could've thought of more exciting ways to spend an evening than huddled around a desk with Ronald Gross, but in terms of achieving the objective at hand, it was worth it.

Analysis: Ronald was a good teacher.

Unlike Brad—who was more interested in hooking up than studying—Ronald had a way of making even the most complex ideas and problems seem simple. During that first evening, he was patient, helpful, and never made me feel like any question was too dumb (and I guarantee you, there were a lot of dumb questions). More than just explaining factoring and linear equations in down-to-earth ways, Ronald also had practical tips that could get my scores up right away; tips relating to things like pacing myself and eliminating answers when possible. And remarkably, what had begun as a cover for the Taker became something I just might be interested in doing. I kind of enjoyed studying with Ronald that week, because for once I was conquering the damn SAT—not the other way around. I was picking myself up by my bootstraps, and I felt good for it.

Come Thursday morning, I called him to confirm our plans for that night. He told me to come by his house around six o'clock.

"I thought we were going to meet right after school?" I asked, confused.

"Yeah, but now I think a little later is better."

"Why?"

He mumbled something unintelligible on the other end of the line, but even without a good reason, I said fine. I figured Ronald didn't want to admit to having something dorky to do beforehand; Mensa meeting or whatever.

"Okay," I said. "I'll do some writing at school and meet you after."

"Oh, good, you'll be hungry then," he chirped.

"What?"

"Nothing. I'll see you at six," he said quickly. "Bye."

And with that he hung up.

In retrospect, I suppose I should have known from the "hungry" comment, but alas, yours truly was a bit dense.

When I got to his house, Ronald was waiting on the stoop, and before I knew it for sure, I smelled it. Smelled what, you ask?

A *date*, that's what.

Ronald's hair was glistening from too much gel, and there was the heavy odor of Old Spice aftershave in the air. I half expected to see my dad pop out of the bushes—Old Spice being the choice of old men—but, no, it was just Ronald. He had a new vintage jacket on (that's what Mrs. G. would call an oxymoron) in gas-station blue with a Standard Oil patch.

Maybe Molly's and my makeover efforts had gone off course.

"Hey," he said as he lifted his chin.

"Hi, Ronald."

I took a step to go inside, but before I even got on the stoop, he popped up and hurried toward a car sitting in the driveway. It was a 1977 blue Pacer with a white racing stripe that I'd only seen out of his parents' garage a handful of times.

"Come on," he said. "Let's grab something to eat."

Something told me to say no—to tell him to order a pizza from Napoli's—but on the other hand, it was Ronald. Even if everything was pointing toward him trying to make a play at a date, I decided I'd give him the benefit of a doubt.

"Is this like, your mom's car?" I asked.

"No, it's mine," he answered. "I saved up."

Okay, now I was baffled.

"If you own a car, why do you take the bus every day? Better yet—why did we walk to Tori's party?"

Was he into some kind of self-torture?

He opened the passenger door for me. "Parents. They have to sign off on my using it twenty-four hours in advance. Their weirdo rules, not mine. Parental-tardation, you know?"

I resisted rolling my eyes.

He made a gesture for me to get in, and a minute later we were out of his driveway and heading down Post Road.

"So where exactly are we going?" I asked, still feeling uneasy about this little . . . excursion.

"The diner," he answered. "You're hungry, right?"

The diner: as in *the* date place in Guilford. This was a train that needed some slowing down.

"First of all, Ronald, I'm not really hungry. Second, let's just be totally clear: this isn't a date. I'm here to study."

He mocked being knifed in the heart before grinning. "I'm not that desperate, you know. I have a project to do later, and my mom doesn't cook, so I eat out a lot."

"Oh, okay," I replied, feeling like a bit of an ass.

"Besides, I'm going to show you something that will make some of the math easier."

Nevertheless, I wasn't so sure I was ready to accept Ronald's reassurances. I mean, was I just supposed to ignore the aftershave, the gel, and the clothes? But once we got on Route 30, any further conversation became virtually impossible. Why is that, you ask? Well, Ronald's Pacer must've been the loudest car ever made. I'm sure it didn't help that half the car was made out of glass, but once the car went over 25 miles an hour, there was no talking—just screaming.

"WHAT ARE YOU GOING TO SHOW ME?" I yelled.

"CAN'T TELL YOU," he shouted back. "IT WILL RU . . . I . . ."

I couldn't understand him—it was that loud.

"WHAT?"

He pointed toward his ears and mouthed, "I can't hear you."

I shook my head and smiled.

"MUSIC?" he yelled.

That part I did get. I nodded.

He pantomimed a box and pointed to the floor in the backseat. Reaching around behind his seat, I grabbed what looked to be a fish tackle box and opened it. But instead of bait, it was full of 8-track cassettes. You know, like on *That '70s Show*? Talk about old school. And as for the selection— it was, um, far from current. Other than the Bob Dylan album, I hadn't heard of a single band.

I made up sign language saying I didn't know which one to pick. He stuck his hand in the box and fished around until finally he pulled out somebody named George Clinton, aka Dr. Funkenstein. On the cover there was a picture of this guy with a huge black Afro, sunglasses, and some psychedelic robe fit for a king.

That's . . . different.

Ronald took the cassette and popped it in a player that hung under the dashboard. He quickly transitioned to side four—Ronald later told me that there are two songs and four sides on an 8-track, hence the name—and the song that came on was called "Bring On Da Funk." And you know what? It didn't sound that bad. Sure, it wasn't exactly the type of music I'd want to listen to while I did my homework, but it was okay. As the song picked up momentum, Ronald began to "funk" out as he drove— moving his body like a man possessed while still managing to stay on his side of the road—and I'd be lying if I didn't say that he looked totally ridiculous. But it was also incredibly funny . . . Funny in the best possible way.

Who knows? I said to myself. *Maybe this is all going to turn out okay.*

How wrong could I have been? Very wrong.

According to Ronald's calculations, it takes Carly, on average, 15 hours of studying with him to get her SAT score up 10 points. At this rate of studying, how many hours does Carly have to study with the Gross in order to improve her score by 300 points?

    (A) 15

    (B) 100

    (C) 200

    (D) 450

    (E) forever

WE'D BEEN SITTING at the diner for fifteen minutes, and I was still waiting for Ronald to say something, anything, related to the SAT.

"They're doing this really cool light show at the Planetarium in a few weeks," he said. "Have you ever been there?"

"No, I haven't," I answered monotone, hoping he might get the hint that we should get down to studying.

"Oh, it's so awesome, you gotta check it out," he continued. "The whole dome has this projection of the cosmos, and they show you all the constellations, like Cassiopeia and Orion's belt and . . ."

I tuned Ronald out and scanned the diner.

There were a lot of kids from GHS hanging out, but I was happy to note that none of my friends were there. When we'd arrived, Ronald had insisted that we get the corner table—Hello, the date table, red flag again!—so just about the last thing I wanted was to see anyone I knew— particularly any of Brad's friends.

". . . and then, at the end of the night," Ronald continued, "they have this laser show where—"

"Maybe we should *order*, Ronald."

He blinked a few times. "Uh, sure."

Seizing control, I flagged down Trudy from across the room. Trudy and Tacy were sixty-year-old twins, and they worked the night shift at the Guilford Diner. They'd been waiting tables there ever since I could remember, and they knew all the families in town. Both were built like weight lifters, and adding to their bordering-on-comical looks, were their short shag haircuts and four-inch platform nurse shoes (Trudy wore white and Tacy wore black, actually—their one distinguishing mark).

Trudy waddled over to our table and snapped her gum.

"Evening, Carly. Ronald." She pulled a pencil out from behind her ear. "What's it gonna be?"

But right when I was about to order, Ronald interrupted.

"I'll have a black-and-white shake, two steak bombs with Swiss cheese instead of American, the curly fries, and . . ." He flipped to the back of the menu. " . . . and Carly will have the macro salad. That's four hundred calories, right?"

Macro salad?

I couldn't speak. It was as if somebody had run me over with a truck. What was he doing?

"Thanks, babe," Trudy clucked before turning my way. "Anything to drink for you?"

"I'll have—"

"She'll have a Diet Coke."

Where did he get off ordering for me? Had the

whole feminist movement passed him by? Furthermore (and possibly worse), never in my life—not even on dates with the biggest meatheads—had somebody just come out and essentially said, "Eat this, you're fat." I stared at Ronald—wishing I could bore holes into his head with my eyes—and he took a notebook out of his backpack and began jotting down a bunch of numbers on some graph paper. He was completely oblivious to what was going on inside me.

I suspected then that I had made a terrible miscalculation. The only thing worse than a dork is a dork with attitude; and obviously my friendly behavior over the last few days had taken root in the worst possible way. With a misplaced sense of entitlement, he was now overreaching—first by planning this mini-date, and second by having the gall to order for me.

Ronnie needed a reality check.

"Excuse me."

"Yeah, what's up?" he asked.

"In case you've been living in a cave your whole life, women can order for themselves."

He shrugged his shoulders. "You said you weren't hungry and I was going to—"

"That's the rudest thing anybody has ever done to

me," I said. It wasn't, actually, but I thought I may as well make him squirm.

He looked surprised. "I'm sorry, I didn't realize . . . um . . . um . . ."

I put my palm toward him and looked away to let him know that, as far as I was concerned, there was no excuse for his actions.

"Carly, I . . ."

Palm.

"You see . . ."

Palm!

"Um . . ."

PALM.

He gave up.

Five silent minutes later, Trudy arrived at our table and put down our meals. In front of Ronald . . . a trough of food . . . and in front of me . . . a tiny plate of green cow grazings. Presumably relieved not to have to talk, Ronald dug into his fries, but I just kept staring down at my salad.

Then, just as I was considering ordering something myself and making peace—otherwise I wouldn't learn a thing that night—the only thing that could've made the situation worse . . . happened.

I think it was Ronald who saw them first, because

mid-bite the blood drained out of his face and he blanched to the color of a corpse. Seeing that something was wrong, I looked over toward the door.

Ohhhhhhhhhh, nooooooo.

It was Brad.

The lacrosse game! The team must've stopped to pick up some food on their way back to school!

I ducked as far into the booth as I could, praying Brad hadn't seen us through the window from the bus, but no such luck. We'd been discovered. Brad, and his ever-present sidekick Rick, sauntered up to our table, and I cringed, knowing how mean-spirited Brad and Rick could be when they egged each other on in their stupid, macho lacrosse way.

"Hey, Brad," I said with a twinkle, hoping that we could skate right by this awkward moment.

No such luck. He just stared at us, sizing up the situation.

"Yo, Brad," Rick taunted. "Gross here is making the moves on your girl."

"Rick, don't be such a doofus. We're studying," I snapped.

Brad was silent, and I could tell that he hadn't decided how he was going to react to finding me at the diner with

Ronald. I kicked myself for not having admitted to Brad earlier that I was studying with Ronald.

"Looks like a date to me," Rick said. "Damn, Gross, you stink like a date."

No matter how awkward *I* felt, it looked like it was a hundred times worse for Ronald. I guess he'd been down this road too many times in his short life—whether it was when Kevin Bagley had dumped a chocolate milk shake on his head (seventh grade), or the hundred or so times Rick had shorted him in gym class. Like Pavlov's dog (Bio 101: the bell rings and the dog salivates, remember?), the mere sight of Rick and Brad sent tremors down poor Ronald's spine.

"Gross, what are you doing?" Brad said.

"Nothing. I mean, we're studying, for the SAT."

Rick snickered. "That can be a good time as long as Carly's daddy don't interrupt." And then he cracked up laughing.

I looked long and hard at Brad. He wasn't supposed to tell anyone about that night—he'd promised!

"Shut up, Rick," Brad commanded. He scratched his chin before grabbing one of Ronald's steak bomb sandwiches. He took a bite.

"Mmmmm, that's a good sandwich," he said, before

tossing the remnants back on Ronald's plate.

"Brad, that's rude," I said.

"Oh, I'm rude?" he growled, turning my way. "I thought you had to stay home and study tonight, so you couldn't come to our game."

I saw that this was about to become a big scene, so I got up and walked out toward the parking lot. Thankfully, Brad followed. At the door I glanced back at Ronald and saw that Rick had grabbed the other sandwich and had begun eating it as well, licking the roll as he went. Ronald was just sitting there—frozen. Part of me wanted to help him, but I couldn't protect Ronald and save my relationship with Brad at the same time. Let's not forget—just in case you think it was cruel of me to leave him alone with Rick—that the little date-monger himself had started this mess by trying to get a little something-something out of our study session.

"What the hell?" Brad shouted, now that we were both in the parking lot.

"Nothing's going on . . . What could possibly be going on?" I said. "And keep your voice down."

"Keep my voice down?"

Brad reddened and glanced back toward the lacrosse bus, where a bunch of his goon teammates—Molly called them the lacrosstitutes—had their noses pressed against the glass, watching our little blowout.

He took a deep breath.

"What's up with the egghead?" he hissed.

"Listen to me for one second, okay? Mrs. G. set this up. Ronald runs the tutorial lab, and apparently he's a genius at the SAT."

"She set up a date with Ronald Gross?" he asked.

"No . . . I mean, yes. She set up a tutoring schedule with him . . . This is his only free time." Hoping to lighten the situation, I cracked a joke. "Ronald can only tutor at night 'cause he's splitting the atom during the day."

Brad smiled thinly, but I could tell he was also still computing—did it add up? He'd probably picked up on Ronald's aftershave and new duds, and though my story sounded right to him, our being at the diner just didn't.

"This is bullshit," he concluded. "I'm leaving." He turned and started striding toward the bus. I grabbed his arm, but he yanked it away and kept walking.

"Brad! Do you really think I'd date Ronald Gross?!" I shouted.

Much to my relief, that seemed to do the trick, because suddenly Brad stopped. Seizing my chance, I ran up to him and wrapped my arms around his neck.

"C'mon, sweetie. Don't be upset."

We stood there like that for a few moments, and gradually he began to calm. And while I wanted Brad to feel better about things, a thought flew into my head: why was it that *I* had to report to Brad where I was all the time, and yet entire nights would go by when Brad didn't let me know where *he* was, or even call me?

But this was a question for another time.

I gave him a light kiss on the lips.

"This isn't over," he said.

"How could you think that I'd cheat on you?"

"There's a lot of things I don't get about us," he grumbled. "Everybody else . . . you know . . . Why don't you just take Lettich's course, like Tori and everybody else?" he continued.

"Fellner said there weren't any spaces left."

"Tell you what," he said in a whisper. "You don't need to worry. Talk to Rick tomorrow at school. He'll hook you up on the SAT."

"What do you mean?"

"Just talk to him."

"I don't understand."

But before I could get any more info out of him, Brad pointed toward the diner and started laughing. I turned.

There was Ronald, in the doorway with my backpack . . . and a to-go bag.

"Gross is carrying your doggie bag," Brad sneered. "Isn't that sweet." And as if on cue, Rick starting barking like a dog behind Ronald.

Considerate of Ronald? Yes. Good timing? No.

I grabbed Brad's arm.

"Brad, I love you," I said low in his ear, "but if you make this boy cry in front of me, I'll never speak to you again."

Brad looked down at me, and in that instant, his face held an odd look of both bemusement and indecision. I wasn't sure what hand I'd just played, but I knew I wasn't bluffing—not at that moment. If you had asked me at the beginning of the week if I would've done that for Ronald, I probably would've said no. Brad and I stared at each other, and though we weren't speaking, we were communicating. I know that much.

Thankfully, he backed off.

"Gross!" he shouted. "She better make the 2400 Club, or my boy Rick and I are coming to get you."

"Uh, that's six hundred and ninety points," Ronald wheezed, nervous.

Brad waved Rick over, and they got back on the

waiting lacrosse bus while Ronald seized his moment of escape and scurried to his car.

I stood there in the parking lot for a moment or so—between Ronald in his car and Brad on his bus—and found myself wanting no part of either one of them.

W HEN I FINALLY got into Ronald's car, he was scribbling what I assumed was a note of apology—do guys write apology notes?—but I couldn't even look at him. If I spoke at that moment I would have screamed, so I remained silent and just stared into the distance. After a minute or so he turned to me.

"Carly, here's—"

"Don't speak, Ronald. Just take me home."

"'Kay."

"'Kay?!" I shouted with an unexpected fury. "Do you know how embarrassing that was? How much trouble you got me into with Brad?"

"Sorry."

He put the car in gear, and we said nothing to

each other the whole way home.

I know I was being a bit harsh—but I couldn't help myself. I was *pissed*. This weasel had conned me into going to the diner with him, not taught me a single thing, and almost ruined my relationship with Brad.

Fortunately, we soon arrived at my house, but before I got out of the car, Ronald thrust his sheet of paper in my hand. In another situation I might have found it cute and touching, but right then I thought it was just plain lame.

"I don't want your apology note."

"Take it," he said.

Relenting, I snatched it from his hand and shoved the paper in my bag.

"I appreciate what you're doing for me, Ronald," I began, "but this was total bull tonight. Where do you get off thinking you're going to take me out on a date?"

He was quiet.

"I'm here to study, Ronald, and you didn't teach me a single thing tonight. The only thing I did learn was that you're no different from any other guy."

And I got out and slammed the door.

That night I sat around and waited for Brad's call. It came at 11:00 P.M., and strangely, we didn't immediately speak about the diner or Ronald Gross. I tried to bring it up—it was, after all, hanging there in the air between us—but when I asked him if he wanted to talk about it, he just said we should roll on. *No biggie.* Part of me knew that we needed to talk about it—Dad always said that the key to a good relationship was being able to talk about anything— but I was too tired to argue about it. We did need to have a little chat about him telling Rick what had happened with my father, but I decided that could wait.

After I hung up, I changed for bed and put on one of Brad's old T-shirts and a pair of boxers. I prepped my bag for the next day, and it was only then that I came across Ronald's note. I was calm enough to look at it now, so I pulled it out. But I quickly discovered that it wasn't a note. It was a series of word problems.

The Diner and the SAT
1. The human body burns 40 calories an hour without exercise. If Carly ate a macro salad, which contained 400 calories, how many hours would it take to burn off her salad?

Well, that's easy, I thought. 400 divided by 40. The answer is 10.

A softball, I know, but I had to smile.

Next question:

2. Brad burns 300 calories an hour playing lacrosse or exercising, and he burns 80 calories an hour when not exercising. At 6 P.M., Brad ate 3000 calories that Ronald ordered. If Brad exercises for 2 hours and then plays Halo (which does not qualify as exercise) with Rick the rest of the night, how many hours will it take for Brad to burn off Ronald's food?

There were two more just like that one.

I worked the problems, and it was amazing how easily I got the answers; even the last one, which was a brain-teaser. Somehow Ronald had made hypothetical story problems—I always had a hard time with those—concrete and real, and now they were more manageable in my mind. I was pretty sure I'd gotten them all right.

Once I was finished with Ronald's problems, I had a long think—on non-SAT matters. A quick glance across the street revealed that the lights in Ronald's room on the second floor were still on, so I climbed out of bed and put on my robe. I'd been mean to Ronald and I had to set things right. Would calling him have been easier? Sure. But as far I knew, Ronald didn't have a cell, and it was definitely too late to call his home number.

I slipped out the front door—the 'rents were already asleep—and barefoot, I padded my way across the street to the side of Ronald's house. At the curb I picked up a few pebbles, but once I was beneath the room with the lights on, poised to throw, I hesitated. That was Ronald's room, wasn't it? In my mind, I tried to retrace my steps through his house the one time I'd been in there, and I was ninety percent sure it was. Yes. It definitely was.

I tossed the first stone, and it pinged harmlessly off the glass. I waited a few beats, but when there was no sign of movement within, I threw another.

C'mon, Ronald.

A shadow moved across the ceiling, indicating that someone was about, and a moment later a figure struggled with the window. But when it opened and a head popped out, it wasn't Ronald.

Uh-oh.

"Mrs. Gross!"

She was all prepped for bed—hair in big rollers, a mud mask on her face, and from my vantage point . . . wearing what appeared to be a cheetah print robe. But, while most parents would be pissed to find someone throwing stones at their window in the middle of the night, Ronald's mother proved to be otherwise.

"Carly!" she gushed. "Hello, darling!"

"I'm soooo sorry," I said. "I got confused with the windows. I thought that—"

"You're looking for Ronnie, sweetie? Let me get him for you! You just stay right there—don't move!"

Before I could finish an apology, she'd ducked back inside, and from within I could hear her calling him.

"Ronnie, Ronnie! Wake up, dear! Carly's here! Ronnie!!"

The light snapped on in the room adjoining Mrs. Gross's, and there were the confused murmurings of a male voice, before I heard him yell, "Mother—don't call me Ronnie!"

I suppressed a giggle as Ronald's window slid open and he looked down at me. He was wearing a retainer.

"Found the problems?" he asked.

"Yes, thank you. I'll have you check them out tomorrow, but I'm pretty sure I got them all right."

"Sweet."

I shifted my weight. "I'm sorry about what I said earlier."

"No worries," he answered. "But I'm sorry about Brad. It was my bad."

"I'll worry about Brad," I said. "You stay focused on the teaching."

He gave me a thumbs-up.

Suddenly Mrs. Gross stuck her head out of her window. "Carly, why don't you come in. I can make you two some hot chocolate, and I'm pretty sure that I have—"

"Mother!" Ronald sighed. "We're fine!"

"Nonsense," she shouted back across the wood siding. "She should come up, and you two can talk."

Ronald looked like he just might spontaneously combust, so I jumped in. "I have to go—but thanks, Mrs. Gross. I'll see you tomorrow . . . *Ron.*"

I overpronounced it so he'd be sure to hear it.

"Well, okay," she said, disappointed. "Good night, Carly. Good night, Ronnie . . . er, *Ron.*"

Her window closed and Ronald mouthed an apology.

I winked at him to say it was okay—and I think he blushed.

The main purpose of the previous chapter was to show that

    (A) Rick Sorenson is a meathead

    (B) Brad sometimes brings out the worst in Carly

    (C) Ronald's an okay guy

    (D) Never trust a boy wearing Old Spice aftershave

    (E) It's bad to rush to judgment

I WAS ON THE HUNT for Rick Sorenson the whole next day at school.

Brad's suggestion that I talk to him about the SAT had been bouncing around the back of my head since the previous night. Could Rick be the Taker? It seemed unlikely in a lot of ways. Rick had never struck me—or *anyone* for that matter—as a mental giant, but maybe he'd found out some secret to acing the SAT. But if he were the Taker, it would actually be a bit of a relief, because Rick would certainly never do anything weird to me afterward—you know, when I had to do whatever the Taker asked—'cause if he did, Brad would kick his ass.

The more I thought about it—and I spent all morning dwelling on it—the more plausible it seemed that Rick could be the Taker. Not the "how" part, necessarily, but the "why" part. Maybe Rick was into me. Hadn't he gotten a little touchy-feely with me a few times at parties? Sure, I'd always figured it was because he'd had a few beers, but maybe it was because he actually liked me. And maybe Rick thought that by helping me on the SAT, he could show me what a good guy he actually was, and not only get my attention, but also my affections.

But one thing about it didn't quite piece together in my mind. If Rick was the Taker, why would he now bother to involve Brad?

I was still on the fence as to whether or not Rick was the Taker, when the alarm went off at school for what was our ninety-ninth fire drill of the year. I've often wondered what the purpose was of all our fire drills—I doubted if anyone would ever believe there *was* a fire at this point—but regardless, it was a great excuse to get out of Mr. Hubble's guilt-inducing ethics class.

Standing in the quad, I scanned the masses of students, looking for Jen or Molly, when I noticed Rick standing alone by the announcement board. I made my way in his direction.

"Another fire drill, huh?" I said, by way of greeting.

"Better than Miss Healy's English class," he answered.

One thing was for sure: if he was into me, he sure had a funny way of showing it. No boy had ever seemed so bored in my company.

"Have you figured out where you're applying to colleges yet?" I asked, searching for a seamless transition into the SAT convo.

"Yeah."

Silence.

"Are you applying to a lot of places?"

"Not really."

It was like trying to get water from a stone. Left with no other choice, I tried a new method. What my dad would call *being straightforward*.

I checked around to make sure no one was within earshot. "Listen, Rick. Brad said that I should talk to you about the SAT."

He snorted and laughed. "Isn't that what you have the Gross for?"

Ha-ha, Monkey Boy. But I restrained myself.

"I'm serious. Brad said you might be able to hook me up . . . in order to . . . you know . . . get a good score."

An indecipherable expression flashed across his face—anger? confusion? bewilderment?—before he shrugged his shoulders.

"I don't know what Brad's talking about."

Now it was my turn to be confused.

"You don't?"

"Nope," he said. "I mean, I'm feeling good about how the next one's going to go for me, but I don't know how I could help you. It's all about studying, I guess."

Studying. Was I imagining it, or was that close to what the Taker had told me to do? But before I could push him further, Rick sort of looked around and then bolted with a quick "later."

If he was on a quest to woo me, he wasn't exactly winning points in my book.

"Miss Biels," I suddenly heard behind me.

I turned around.

Oh my God.

"Hi, Mr. Fellner."

How long had he been there?

"How's your studying going?"

I recovered and smiled brightly—the very portrait of a diligent student with a glorious future. "I'm working very hard."

He nodded to himself, but I couldn't really gauge what he was thinking. You see, even though it was the beginning of November, he was wearing dark sunglasses. It was kind of weird. Sure, it was a sunny day, but still. I began to suspect that Mr. Fellner was quite vain.

Had he overheard my conversation with Rick?

"You may have heard the announcement in assembly on Tuesday, but I wanted to bring it to your attention personally," he droned. "Mr. Lettich is giving a talk to the juniors this afternoon about the SAT prep course he offers."

"That's right. Yes, I do remember."

Actually, I didn't.

"Obviously, you're not a junior, and to be perfectly frank, I'm no more optimistic than I was last time we spoke about your being able to get into his current course, but I think it would be worthwhile for you to go. It would give you a sense of what his course entails. And perhaps it might even inspire you to work harder."

"I think that's a terrific idea. Thanks, Mr. Fellner."

Don't you hate sucking up to teachers?

The "all clear" bell sounded, and disappointed students began to shuffle back into the building.

"It's at three o'clock," he said. "Make sure you're there."

I said I would and, among the hordes, began the trek back toward the entrance to the school. For a split second—in the distance—I thought I saw Brad . . . with Tori Clemens. But as the crowd cleared and I got a better view, neither one of them were anywhere to be seen.

Maybe I just imagined it.

SURVIVING THE SAT: TIP #4:

TUTORS

● ●

Many parents will hire you a tutor (or get you into a tutor's class) to help you prepare for the SAT. Though by no means a necessity, studying with a tutor/class can be a big help in pushing scores to a desirable level. Much as with section #2, where guidance counselors were discussed, extreme care must go into selecting the type of tutor that best fits with your studying methods and personality. Most tutors tend to fall into the following categories:

THE FASCIST JERK: You may think that you're studying for the SAT, but spending time with this tutor feels more like you are serving a life sentence in a maximum security prison. Relentlessly demanding, never cracking a smile, and constantly acting as if you are wasting his/her time, you often wonder how it is that your parents are, in fact, paying for you to be treated so poorly.
Recommended for students who: have served in juvenile detention centers; are thinking of entering the armed

forces; or particularly enjoy the writing of the Marquis de Sade.

THE NITPICKER: Failing ever to see the "big picture," this tutor will spend an entire tutoring session going over one—yes, ONE—type of problem. You will almost surely be bored to tears as this teacher waxes on about subjunctive clauses, right triangles, or conjunctions—for an entire hour. Sure, you're likely to become the expert at your school on the aforementioned subjects, but each section on the SAT does have fifty questions, and you may not ever get to the forty-nine other topics that almost certainly will be covered.

Recommended for students who: only have difficulties on one section of the SAT; have a lifetime to study; or find reading the footnotes in the back of textbooks a fascinating pastime.

THE SNOB: Usually an undergraduate from a prestigious nearby college, this tutor aced the SAT with ease, and thinks that anyone who cannot, must be of lesser genetic stock. Prepare for subtly condescending remarks: *C'mon, you learned this in the eighth grade*—and outright put-downs—*Oh, you did say you went to a public school, didn't you?* These types of tutors can be helpful in terms of preparation for the exam, but arm yourself against their snarky attitude.

Recommended for students who: have experience with older/MIT-bound siblings; agree that attending an Ivy League college makes you an intrinsically superior human being; or are aspiring snobs themselves.

I WAS TEN MINUTES late getting to Mr. Lettich's presentation, and seeing that the only free seats were in the front few rows, I leaned against the wall in the back of the auditorium. There was a pile of fancy-looking brochures sitting on the floor by the door, and I picked one up. On the front, there was a picture of Mr. Lettich leading a group of impossibly happy, ethnically diverse students up a hill, with a caption beneath that read GET TO THE TOP.

"Knowledge. Knowledge is power," Mr. Lettich said. "And I'm here to offer you *power*."

Yeah. I guess you could say that he took himself pretty seriously.

"The power to control your future. Your life. Your destiny. With knowledge." He paused here and eyeballed the crowd. "And you have to ask yourself—do you have what it takes? Are you willing to make the sacrifices? Are you prepared to do what has to be done . . . to be a winner?"

There was silence in the room while he let his words set in. Half the room nodded, like sheep to the slaughter, while the other half sat there mute and stupefied—the enormous jaws of the SAT chomping before them.

"My course isn't for everyone. I'm very selective. But if you are accepted into my three-month program, I personally guarantee that your scores will go up two hundred points."

Murmurs of interest rippled through the crowd.

Lettich started giving examples of his former students—how their scores had changed, where they'd gone to college, and so on—and I watched as the better part of the room started salivating. I have to admit that I was pretty impressed as well. I mean, how could you not be? Two hundred points. Like, wow!

But how was he able to promise that? Was he really that good with the SAT? Sure, he'd been a good history teacher, but it didn't necessarily follow that he'd suddenly become some SAT guru. There isn't even a history section on the SAT! But who was I to question? If he could make that big a difference, of course it would be good to be in the course.

"If you want to be part of the few. The proud. The elite," he continued, ripping off the slogan of the Marines, "then my course is the right course for you."

Somebody raised their hand with a question, and it was right then that I heard my cell beep with a text. I slipped my phone out of my pocket and opened it.

JEN: What a loser

Was she talking about Lettich? I scanned the audience but didn't spot her. The phone beeped again.

JEN: Back left

I turned my head and surveyed the back of the auditorium. There, with her finger in her throat, making a fake gagging motion, was Jen. Obviously she was just as enamored of Lettich as I was.

CARLY: Why r u here?
JEN: Inquiring minds want to know

Of course. For her investigation. I should've guessed that she'd be here.

"And now I'm going to demonstrate how the class works," Lettich announced. "Is there a volunteer who'd like to come up onstage and work with me for a few minutes?"

A few bold souls raised their hands—I surely wouldn't have volunteered, for fear of getting the answer wrong and looking dumb—and Lettich pointed to someone down in front.

"Why don't you come up, young lady."

I couldn't help but laugh to myself when I saw who it was. Rachael Harrison. Naturally he would pick her. She'd been a bit of a late bloomer, but oh, had she filled out in the last year, and almost overnight her social stock had gone from sell to buy. Her breasts had gotten so big that she'd nearly knocked herself out doing jumping jacks. There was little doubt in my mind that she'd get into Lettich's class, no matter how dumb she was.

Across the auditorium, someone read my mind, and my phone beeped again.

JEN: Tell your dad to put his money in breast implants—that's the only sure ticket to L's class.

Lettich gave Rachael a sample problem to do, but by this point I was starting to tune out. I'd gotten the gist of what Lettich was about, and standing there watching him ogle some junior seemed like a big waste of time. Besides, the Terminator wasn't around, so I could just tell him that I'd been there. This is what we call *Time Management.*

CARLY: I'm outta here
JEN: Wait 4 me

"What a blowhard," Jen said as we walked across the quad toward the parking lot.

"Yeah. He's like the evil Dr. Phil."

Jen chuckled.

"Did you find anything out from the talk?" I asked.

She waved Lettich's brochure. "It's all right here. This reduces the research I have to do on him, because he practically lays it all out in black and white. It's perfect."

"Cool."

"How's your studying going?" she asked.

"Oh, you know. It's gripping as always. I'll be so happy when all this SAT stuff is finished."

As we walked in silence for a few moments, I heard the lacrosse team chanting in unison as they did their warm-ups. Lacrosse was *the* sport at Guilford High, and they had their own clubhouse and practice field about two hundred yards from the main building. When Brad and I had first started dating, in fact, I'd often sat in the bleachers and done my homework while they scrimmaged, but by now I was over it.

I thought then about walking over and giving a wave to Brad. I hadn't seen him since the drama at the diner . . . whose fault that was, I couldn't really say . . . but a moment later I decided just to keep walking.

Jen cocked her head. "Is Ronald Gross tutoring anyone else?"

"I don't think so, but I don't know for sure."

She made a note on the back of Lettich's brochure.

"Why? Are you going to put Ronald on *the board*?"

I hadn't been able to sneak back into the room off the offices of *The Guilfordian* to examine "the board" since I'd been in there last. Oh, I'd tried. But the door was always locked.

Jen pursed her lips. "I'm not sure. I mean, he is a member of the 2400 Club, so he should be, and yet, I can't really imagine Ronald Gross helping anyone cheat. It's just not his MO."

I agreed with her.

"Either way, it wouldn't matter," Jen continued, "because I have a new approach for cracking my story."

"Oh, yeah?"

"You see, rather than trying to find the ringleader—which was like looking for a needle in a haystack—I've decided to narrow my investigation."

"What do you mean?"

We arrived at Jen's Jeep, and she unlocked the back so she could toss her bag in.

"Well, I realized that I was trying to cover too much. My father told me once that when you're researching an article—just like when you're doing a scientific experiment—you have to decide what it is that you're going to observe or monitor."

"Uh-huh."

"Because, let's face it: the Taker, or whatever you want to call him—or *her*—isn't just going to show his face. He's smart. He's been doing this for a while, and he has the routine of staying secret totally down. But the students who need to get their scores up are the ones who are acting out of the norm. And more than likely can lead me to him."

"So you're like, spying on students?" I asked, shocked—for a lot of reasons.

"I'm not *spying*, I'm watching," she explained with gathering enthusiasm. Jen talked about her articles the way some girls talk about their prom. "I came up with a list of the ten students most likely to cheat; students who under-achieved on the SAT, but also have access to money in some way. The money part is important, because no one's going to help you cheat unless you pay them, right?"

I nodded.

"Sometime soon, one of these students is going to slip up; they're going to do something obvious, say something stupid or whatever, and I'm going to be there to expose them." She put her hands on her hips, impressed with herself. "Pretty smart, right?"

"Sure," I answered, like she was a regular Nancy Drew. A beat later, I laughed a little more nervously than I would've liked and then blurted out, "So am I on the list?"

Jen fixed me with a stare. "You were. But I took you off."

It was like getting kicked in the stomach.

"I was?"

She nodded and raised her eyebrows, before grabbing my arm and leaning close. "J.K., Carly! Totally just kidding!"

I made a goofy expression that suggested I thought I was stupid for having been so gullible, but inside I was still reeling from the thought that Jen might be investigating *me*.

She kissed me on the cheek—a Judas kiss?—and

hopped into her car. As she drove away, I still felt my stomach twisting. Despite what she'd said, part of me suspected that I might still be on the list.

I reminded myself that if I wanted to keep Jen off my trail, I had to keep studying with Ronald.

I NEVER DID GET to see the board again, and more important, I never made any further progress with Rick Sorenson. I made a couple of overtures, but Rick only got weirder and weirder about it. Brad was zero help, because, when I sent him a text that night to tell him how Rick had blown me off, he'd replied:

BRAD: Can't talk—at gym—gotta do chest

Gotta do chest?

And you know what was even more lame? He never brought it up after that, and frankly, I felt awkward mentioning it again. I mean, shouldn't *he?* Brad had no excuse for not helping me this time, because he knew how stressed

I was about the SAT. But that's just how it goes with Brad, I told myself. Eventually I came to the conclusion that there wasn't anything real to be gotten from Rick—that Brad had just said that in the heat of the moment to get me away from Ronald. I crossed Rick off the list of possible suspects for the Taker.

And so, day after day passed; studying with Ronald (who was proving himself to be a terrific tutor), getting ready for the school's practice SAT, and gradually feeling more and more isolated from everyone. I saw more of Ronald than anyone else during that period—even my parents—and I remember thinking to myself that this so wasn't how I expected my senior year to turn out. Sure, Jen and I would IM late at night—and of course Molly and I had our mornings together, but something had changed. I guess it was me.

Wiped out from a long but incredibly useful night of studying with Ronald, I arrived home and found my mother in the kitchen, cleaning up after a late dinner. I plopped down on one of the stools, and Mr. Biggles came over and nuzzled at my ankles.

"How's it going with the Gross boy?" my mother asked as she offered me some cranberry juice.

"With Ronald?" I corrected. *Hello, he has a name.* "It's going well, really well."

"Glad to hear it."

I picked up Mr. Biggles and sat him in my lap. Simply running my hand through his coat buoyed my spirits, and I smiled to myself as he rested his head on my leg. Sometimes dogs just have a way of making you feel better, you know?

"Your father and I are very proud of you," I heard my mother say as she put the last of the dishes away. "Of how hard you're working."

You always hope your parents will say something like that to you, but I was in no position to enjoy it. *Proud of what?* Of keeping a deep cover while the Taker prepares to do my bidding?

"Thanks."

She crossed to me and put her hand on my arm. "When this is all done—no matter what happens—you and I will go have a girls' day in the city. Just the two of us. We'll go to Bliss! Sound good?"

I nodded without looking up.

She said good night, and I was alone with Mr. Biggles.

After a few minutes, I pulled my phone from my bag. Sometimes when you're feeling down, you just need to hear someone say I love you—someone other than your parents, because they have to love you, right?—and I dialed Brad. He answered after a few rings.

"Hey."

"Hi, sweetie. Am I waking you up?"

"Yeah," he said with a trace of irritation in his voice. "We have morning practice tomorrow so I figured I'd crash early. What's up?"

I hesitated a beat. Earlier in our relationship, Brad had always been so sweet when I called, no matter what hour of the night. Always saying how good it was to hear my voice, how much he missed me; but recently . . .

"I wanted to hear your voice," I whispered. "I think I'm just getting really burned out with all this SAT stuff."

"I told you you were spending too much time with the Gross. That'll bring anybody down."

The diner—ridiculously—was still a bit of a sore subject.

"It's not about Ronald. It's everything else. My parents. Fellner. And . . ." I trailed off, almost saying "the Taker." "Maybe I need to take a break from studying," I covered, but I knew that wasn't the answer.

Brad didn't say anything until he managed the disappointingly minimal, "Yeah. A break probably is a good idea."

My spirits perked up. "Hey! Why don't we go do something fun one night next weekend. We could go into the city—it could be romantic."

"I hate the city," he grunted, as it sounded like he turned his head into the pillow. "Let's go to the Pinewood party at Jay's."

"Yeah, I guess that could be fun."

Watching Brad play quarters with meatheads—*not* fun.

"His parents are going to be out of town. Maybe we could spend the night there."

Needless to say, my parents would never agree to that, nor was I sure that I wanted to put myself in that situation.

"That could be an option," I offered. "It's just . . . I haven't gotten to see much of you lately. I mean, just us. One on one."

"You've been so busy studying," he said.

"I know. I know."

I didn't know what to say next. There was an awkward silence—just the faint buzz of a cell-to-cell connection—and I couldn't tell if his silence was because he was falling asleep or if he was annoyed.

"Will you come to Young Poets Night?" I finally asked. "It's this Friday—it would mean a lot to me if you were there."

Brad sighed, signaling that he was, in fact, very much awake. "You know that's not my thing."

"Please?" And I instantly despised myself for sounding

so whiny. Deep down, though, I needed some sort of raft to know that our relationship was on safe footing.

"Okay," he finally yielded. "I have a game in the afternoon. I'll swing by after."

"Thanks, baby."

"I gotta go, Carly. I'm worked."

"Of course. Sweet dreams."

"'Night." And hc hung up.

I sat there for I don't know how long, staring at my phone, trying to decide if things really were on shaky ground with Brad, or if I was just imagining it. Maybe I was just dumping all my anxiety about the Taker on Brad. Isn't that what they call "projecting" in psych class? But shouldn't I trust what I'm feeling? I was so confused—by everything—that I couldn't tell up from down anymore.

I shuddered, and in my lap Mr. Biggles looked up at me with dark, worried eyes.

MRS. G. HAD established the final Friday of every month as Young Poets Night—Guilford High's version of the Beat poetry scene. (Ask your English teacher who the Beats were—guaranteed full grade inflation just for asking!) In reality, it was an evening of poetry, monologues, and rap (sans DJ), and any students who had original short stories, three-minute plays, or even some rhymes, could air their material. The rappers and spoken word folks dominated the night, but Mrs. G. insisted that the literary people get their props as well.

And don't let me catch you thinking to yourself that it sounds lame—'cause it isn't. A lot of the stuff that people perform is really cool. Then again, if I told you that, when the lacrosse team has a game, the Young Poets Night is sparsely attended, I'm sure you wouldn't be surprised. All in all, there were about twenty people in the audience that night: nineteen of whom were getting extra credit in Mrs. G.'s sophomore English class. And the twentieth was my dad. He always came to my readings, even if we were in a fight about something dumb like the SAT, or Brad. I guess you could say he is really supportive like that, and truth is, I am always grateful for it.

That's a belated shout-out to you, Pops!

Mrs. G. knew the owner of Beans, our local coffee joint, and although they had an open mike night on Fridays at 8 P.M., Gracie let us hold court from 5 to 7; or until the real performers showed up. The place was dark and cozy, and kind of cool in that old-school jazz way. There were pictures of Ginsberg and Whitman, and of course Dylan, Springsteen, Cobain, and so on. On our night, the freaky regulars who sat there all day drinking Turkish coffees and reading big fat books by people like Marx, Sartre, and Nietzsche (sooooo not my bag), politely moved to the edges so the sons and daughters of the next generation could kick some ass.

Since I was a senior and cochair of *The Mighty Pen* (our literary magazine), I got to choose my place on the program. Despite my better judgment, I was reading a poem

I'd written after my meeting with the Taker. In retrospect, it may have been a confession of sorts, but at the time, I thought I was just shouting at the world.

I'd put myself up last and right after Martha Q.—Guilford High's only lesbian rapper. She had a boulder on her shoulder instead of a chip, but I thought she was great. Her poetry took on everyone and everything—racism, sexism, Republicans, Democrats—and a braver girl I hadn't met at Guilford. When Martha delivered "the word" (as she liked to call it) she carried the weight of a preacher and the song of a siren, all wrapped up in a seismic mix of rhyme and poetry. She was *really* good. She also brought with her the L-Crew (their name, not mine), a small group of outspoken lesbians at GHS who didn't hesitate to show their support for their friends. They were incredibly loud. Nobody with half a brain wanted to read after Ms. Q., because she was an impossible act to top. But I'd chosen to do that very thing because I wanted to give Brad as much time as possible to get there.

I pulled back the curtain from the wings and looked out into the audience.

I spotted Dad right away because he was sitting front and center, double-thumbing on his BlackBerry, seemingly unmoved by Martha's rant against the older white male.

But the person I was really hoping to see was nowhere to be found.

Brad hadn't showed.

Sadness and concern crept into my shoulders, and I stared down at the wood plank flooring. How could he have bailed on coming? Brad's skipping Young Poets Night was not unusual in itself (in our year of dating, Brad had only come once to hear me read), but I'd made a big point of wanting him to be there this time, and he'd ignored it. What had happened to us?

Just as I was about to duck backstage to prepare to read, however, the front door opened and in he came.

But it wasn't Brad. It was Ronald.

He stuck out like a girl on a football team. He was wearing khakis (thankfully not the ones with pleats) and a blue oxford shirt with a button-down collar. Credit to him, he'd nixed the gel, and his wavy black hair fell off to the side in a natural sort of unkempt way. If I hadn't known what a true geek he was, I'd swear he had been styled to look "geek chic," and were the room a little darker, you might just have mistaken him for Tobey Maguire in *Spider-Man*. I hadn't mentioned anything to Ronald about Young Poets Night, but he was there just the same.

"All right y'all," I heard Martha announce at the

microphone. "Here's the soul searcher herself . . . Carly Biels!"

My heart jumped. "Soul Searcher" was Martha's nickname for me, but between being upset about Brad not being there and feeling oddly thrown by Ronald just walking in, I was not prepared to deliver on the promise of anything soul-searching. Steeling myself, I drew the curtain back and walked onstage.

My dad whooped and clapped loudly, and I tamped down with my right hand as I walked past him, but that of course only egged him on to clap louder. I stepped to the podium, and as silence took hold in the room, I composed myself by taking two deep breaths. After a moment, I looked at my poem. It was entitled HEART.

" A Pump? That 's all it is, girl.
No more, no less.
It doesn 't make a love song.
It isn 't lost, broken, longing.
Heart of cheater,
Heart of champion,
Heartless bastard is what he is. . . .

You don 't have heart, young lady—

You never will.
' You gotta have heart. '
(I sang this ironically)

What we 've lost is
Always safe in our hearts,
But what we want
Is always there too. Yeah,
Baby it 's a whole universe. . . .

Who we are is never hidden,
What we want is to be alive,
To be in love, free of love.

Heart, pump, love, lost;
Girl you 've got it all
And nothing at all. "

That was it.

To be honest I still don't know what it means, except that at that moment I was lonely, scared, and right out there on the edge. The Taker was in there—big time. Brad was in there, and I suppose Ronald was also. Mostly though, it was me churning through my emotions about them . . . about everything. That's what's great about writing—sometimes it doesn't add up to something, but it still says everything you couldn't.

When I finished reading, there was silence for the longest time . . . and then . . . stunningly . . . an eruption of clapping.

Wow.

As I walked offstage, Mrs. G. hurried over to the mike and said thank you to everyone for coming while the sophomore English students all bolted for the door. Down in front, my dad waved good-bye, and I gave him a thankful nod. Dad and I have a deal, you see. When he comes to my readings, he has to leave right after and not embarrass me any further, and he always sticks to it. I highly recommend this arrangement, because it lets your parents see what you do—which *is* nice—but it also preempts any potential awkward moments. Ladies, take note.

I grabbed my stuff from behind the curtain and waved good-bye to Mrs. G., who applauded again. Clearly she dug my poem. When I looked around the room, however, Ronald was nowhere to be found. I guess he split.

But as I walked out the door and into the parking lot— thanks to the loudest car in Guilford—I realized he hadn't left.

"Hey!" Ronald shouted from the driver's seat of the Pacer.

"I thought we weren't meeting until later."

"Yeah, we did say nine o'clock, but I thought we should get an early jump on things," he offered. "Tomorrow's your big practice exam, after all."

"I have plans."

That was only partially true. I'd had plans if Brad had shown up, that is, and obviously, that hadn't happened. On the other hand, I didn't want Ronald to think that my life revolved around him, even if it felt like it did.

"That was nice," he said.

"What was nice?" I snapped back.

"Your poem. It was cool."

I softened. "You liked it?"

"Yeah—very Plathian, I think."

Plathian!! A word I'd never heard spoken before, but one that every young girl who has ever picked up a pen wants to hear. Ronald compared me to Sylvia Plath! If you don't know who she is, drop this book, go to the library, and get *The Bell Jar*. *The Catcher in the Rye*—that's for the boys. But *The Bell Jar*—it's for us. Get it, read it, e-mail me. We'll talk.

"Thanks," I gushed. "That dark, huh?"

"But that's good."

"Yeah, that's good." It was around then that everything that had been upsetting me seemed to evaporate. The fact that it was Friday night and I had to study for the SAT—that the Taker was out there looming—that Brad hadn't shown up—all of it disappeared. I felt kind of tongue-tied. "Um, so studying. Your house?"

Ronald smirked. "I think we've seen enough of my mom lately."

I laughed.

"I think we should stick to my plan," he said.

"Plan? So where, the diner?" I asked. My voice must have quivered with fear, because his face dropped.

"No . . . no more Guilford haunts," he answered, shaking his head. "I learned my lesson."

"Okay, then. Where?"

"Just trust me," he said. "About everything."

He sounded so sure, so clear-eyed, that in that instant, I caught sight of something in Ronald: a flash of the future. A glimpse of a young man beneath the exterior of an awkward boy—and a vision of who he would become one day in the not-too-distant future.

"Okay."

And I got in.

Carly is in a car going 50 mph, driving due north out of Guilford. If she travels north for 45 minutes and then travels west for another 10 minutes at a speed of 30 mph, what will she find?

    (A) Timbuktu

    (B) A pot of gold

    (C) Connecticut's favorite redneck hangout

    (D) True love

    (E) A shallow grave

As WE DROVE, Ronald popped in *One Nation Under a Groove* by a band called (what else?) Funkadelic. We cruised north up Route 77, and Guilford proper disappeared behind us in the rearview mirror.

Where were we going?

After a bit, we passed I-80 heading north through the farms of North Guilford and Durham before we got to North Durham, a small town in the center of the state that was about forty minutes from the Guilford Green, but might as well have been halfway around the world. North Durham was most famous for being the home of Bob's Surplus Jeans, and if you haven't heard of Bob's, don't worry—nobody outside of Connecticut has either.

Eventually, Ronald turned off onto what seemed to be the main drag at a small, hand-painted sign that said CODY'S. Pavement quickly gave way to dirt, and we drove through *the woods*—yes, the woods—for about half a mile. Just as I was starting to worry that I was being taken to some abandoned cabin deep in the middle of nowhere, like in *The Texas Chainsaw Massacre*, the driveway opened into a large gravel parking lot. From the collection of pickups and El Caminos—some brand-spanking new, some old and rusting—that were parked along the perimeter of the lot, it was clear where we were:

Redneck country.

Today, looking back, I can say that with pride—but at the time, it was a different matter.

At the end of the lot, I spotted a large wooden building that had a sort of log cabin look about it. There was a sputtering 1950s neon sign that read CODY'S DUCKPINS and hung askew on the front porch, below which were a long line of motorcycles, or what somebody in the know would more appropriately call "hogs." They were obviously bad-ass bikes, ridden by bad-ass men. You know, the kinds of guys who date chicks who wear leather bras?

I'll admit it. I was a little nervous. Actually . . . I was terrified.

"Is this like, a bar?"

Ronald smiled. "Yeah."

I played it cool. If he wasn't worried, I sure wasn't going to cop to feeling panicked. But I also knew I wanted to get the hell out of there.

"I can't . . . I mean, I don't have an ID."

"Don't worry, it's a bowling alley, too—and we're here to bowl. And learn . . . and relax."

We got out of the Pacer and walked toward the building. Too scared to even look up, I fell in, mouselike, behind Ronald. By the front door, there were a couple of gargantuan bikers who looked like grizzly bears, and as we passed, Ronald—surely taking leave of his senses—gave them a chin nod.

But you know what's crazy? They chinned back like they knew him! Okay, had we just entered a parallel universe where Ronald was the motorcycle king?

Inside, there were even more bikers in leather vests and jean jackets, along with tough-looking construction types in well-worn boots (in here, Timberlands were worn for practicality). Cody's had a 1950s look to it, but not in that faux, Johnny Rockets way. It was a relic from another age. According to the national landmark plaque on the foyer wall that I studied rather than meet anyone's eye, it was built in 1952 and was "an excellent example of mass-produced modernism"—whatever that meant.

Behind a chrome counter and standing underneath a sign that read SORRY NO CAPPUCCINO, stood a tiny woman of about fifty in leather pants. She looked tough—like she hadn't been given a thing in her life and wasn't about to give a thing to anybody else—and had a presence that said I own this place. That, plus the fact that the back of her T-shirt said "*I Own This Place*," gave her away. I assumed she must be Cody herself.

Ronald walked up to her and asked for shoes and a lane.

"What size for Princess Preppie?" she zinged.

Ronald looked to me and I told her I was a size six.

She nodded and then glanced at Ronald. "You got a different bird every week, kiddo?"

My head snapped up. Had I misheard or had this woman just suggested that Ronald brought lots of girls here?

He blushed. "I, umm, I . . . no."

"Ronald, you're so easy," she cackled.

With glee, she slammed two pairs of shoes onto the counter, along with a sheet for scoring, and just as we were about to walk away . . . she winked at me. Okay, what was I doing here?

I was in North Durham, Connecticut—aka Backwater, USA.

I was in a bowling alley populated by bikers and their lady friends.

A five foot two leather pant–wearing woman in her fifties had just winked at me.

And it was entirely possible that Ronald Gross was Guilford's unknown gigolo.

Desperate for some connection to reality, I slipped out my cell, but there was still no call from Brad. Not even a text to say "hi," or tell me how the game went, or ask me how I did at my reading.

Ronald and I weaved our way through a group of bikers, and remarkably, they all seemed to know Ronald, and more chins were exchanged. Landing on lane number nine, Ronald sat down at the scorer's table and told me to go first.

To be totally honest—I wasn't exactly raring to go. For starters, I really didn't see how this related to the SAT. Secondly, I hadn't bowled since Julie Berkowitz's ninth-grade bowling party, where (in one of my less graceful moments) I'd dislocated my thumb when I'd failed to release the massive sixteen-pound pink ball that I'd insisted on using because it was the cutest thing I'd ever seen. Then again, there didn't seem to be any threat of a repetition of that feat, because none of the balls at Cody's had any holes. I was baffled.

"There aren't any holes?"

Ronald shook his head. "It's duckpin. You just roll them."

Go-o-ot ittttttt.

I picked up one of the melon-size balls—now feeling like this was the stupidest thing ever—and walked to the line. Feebly, I tossed it down the lane, and the ball landed with a thud and rolled very slowly until the lip of the gutter sucked it in.

"Is this necessary, Ronald?"

"Yes," he said, ignoring my pout, "but if you don't want to roll, that's fine. Just keep score. Do you know how?"

I shook my head.

Ronald sat me down and showed me the box and the basics. Somehow I doubted that this would show up on the SAT, but I kept my mouth shut and scored his first game.

I'm not sure how to tell you this next part, but when Ronald began to bowl . . . a remarkable thing happened. People actually stopped and watched. His motion was fluid—almost ballet-like. It sounds ridiculous, I know, but it's true. He whirled his arm around with speed and power—like a fan on high—and when the ball hand came around, it released into the lane as if his arm and the wood were one, the ball firing across the distance in a seamless transition and slamming into the pins with the destructive force of a jackhammer.

Duckpin—I eventually learned—is bowled with balls slightly bigger than a softball. They weigh eight pounds, and you grip them in your palm and just whip them down the lane. The pins are short and squat (hence the name), and are aligned in the same formation as regular bowling pins, except closer together. Strikes are far more rare than in regular bowling—Ronald explained all this, in case you're wondering—and your chances of bowling a strike in duckpin are about one-sixth that of regular bowling. I didn't know this then, but duckpin bowling hardly exists outside of Connecticut and Massachusetts, and it was quickly disappearing here as well. Cody's was the last duckpin alley in Connecticut.

As people gathered around us, marveling at Ronald, I'll admit it: I felt a little pride. And though the evening may have started at Young Poets Night, seeing Ronald bowl was the most poetic experience of the night. Art, duckpin, and Ronald Gross—I know the terms may not go together naturally, but in this case, they did. It was as pure as any poem I'd ever read.

"You got it tonight, Ronbo," piped a large, hairy dude in an Indian Motorcycles T-shirt.

"Thanks, Pete," Ronald replied.

Pete?

Ronald polished off his fourth spare in five frames, and the man he called Pete walked up and sat next to me at the scorer's table. He was easily over six foot five, and must have weighed close to three hundred pounds. His arm was sleeved out—i.e., tattooed from top to bottom—and his biceps were larger than Brad's legs.

Be cool, Carly.

"Why don't you take another whack at it?" Pete said.

Um, was he talking to me? He was! I must have turned white, because he laughed.

"The name's Pete," he said, holding out a hand the size of a catcher's mitt.

I shook it—it was warm and gentle. "Hi. I'm Carly."

"Give it a try."

"I'd be embarrassed," I said. "I'm not very good."

"Embarrassment—not allowed here," Pete declared. "Note the old gal still sporting leather." He pointed toward Cody.

I laughed.

"Good point. Okay—you keep score."

He chinned me, and I got up and grabbed a ball.

Ronald adjusted my hand and grip, before demonstrating how a duckball was thrown and how to generate power. For a few minutes he waxed poetic about the physics of the game, its geometry, and how power is created. It's strange, what passion can do. Unlike when Brad talked about lacrosse, I was actually interested in what Ronald had to say. More important, Ronald starting drawing correlations to different types of SAT problems, and I finally saw the point of the night.

After a few flimsy attempts, unbelievably I started to get the hang of it. I began to relax and think of each roll as a performance piece, as a little poem about physics, about the fluidity of movement, just like the beauty of words strung together in an Emily Dickinson poem: economical but powerful. On the eighth frame, I rolled my first spare, and then on the tenth, I wowed Ronald with a strike.

"Piece of cake." I high-fived Ronald.

Then Pete got up and put his fist out. I was confused for a second, but then I put out mine and we bumped knuckles. I guess I must have passed some kind of initiation.

"Nice work, little lady."

Pete turned to Ronald. "Hey, Ronbo. You gotta minute to look at my bike?"

Ronald knew how to fix bikes, too?

Ronald glanced at me as if to say *I won't leave you here*, don't worry.

"Go ahead, it's cool," I told him, and the two of them went outside.

Left to my own devices, I watched the other bowlers for a few minutes, and then I got up and walked around. I noticed Old Leather Pants keeping an eye on me, but it was definitely a protective thing. On his way out with Pete, Ronald had stopped at the bar and whispered something in her ear, and since then, I'd felt her watchful gaze, and by extension, Ronald's. It felt nice—to be both set free and watched. That's what Mrs. G. calls a paradox. But isn't that what we all want? To be cared for and to be free? That's love. And wasn't that what I was trying to say in "Heart"? My mom and dad had no sense of balance—it was watch watch watch Carly. No freedom. No trust. With Brad, it was all freedom, for me and for him. There were no obligations and no strings. But in many ways, that was just as bad.

How was it that someone like Ronald Gross had led me to all these revelations?

A little after ten, I wandered to the front door and looked out the window to see if I could find Ronald. He was stripped down to his T-shirt—for all of his good attributes, there was no danger of Ronald becoming the next Calvin Klein model—and he'd climbed underneath Pete's bike. I stepped onto the porchlike area and stood, just watching the two of them. Pete and Ronald were from opposite ends of the universe; a biker who probably owned a plumbing supply company and a kid who was going to go to Princeton or MIT to study math with the greatest minds on earth. What could they have in common?

Respect, I guess.

Ronald slid out from underneath the bike. He had some oil smudges on his left cheek, and his T-shirt was disheveled and hanging out of his khakis. I walked up to the two them.

"Hey," I said.

"We're done," Ronald said as he brushed himself off. "Sorry it took so long."

Pete gave Ronald a pound on the back and said thanks.

"That should hold it till you get it to someone who really knows what they're doing," Ronald said to him.

I said good-bye to Pete, too, and we walked back inside. In our absence, the bowling alley had transformed into a phantasmagoric show of white strobe lights and projected red hearts dancing along the walls. They were playing this Sinatra tune my grandmother used to listen to. "Strangers in the Night."

"Wow."

"Late-night bowling," Ronald explained. "It's like a couples thing."

"I can see that."

Ronald looked at his watch, and then, like Cinderella, announced we had to go. He walked back to our lane and started taking off his bowling shoes.

"Don't you want to roll one more game?" I asked, hoping he'd say yes.

He looked at me questioningly.

"It's okay," I added.

There was a long pause, and he looked into my eyes. It was surreal, because I felt like we were being pulled somewhere, but before we could find out where that was, some-thing clicked in his mind and the light in his eyes went out.

"Not tonight."

I shoved down my disappointment. "That's cool."

Our moment passed, he grabbed our stuff and walked back to the bar. He handed Old Leather Pants our shoes and asked her how much we owed her.

She checked out his scorecard. "Nice game, Ronald. That'll be fifteen dollars."

"I should pay for that, Ronald," I offered.

He looked at me for a few seconds.

"Let me," he said. "Let me pay for this. Okay?"

I nodded.

We left Cody's Duckpins and didn't speak until we got in the car. I grabbed the box of 8-tracks, but he waved them off and handed me a clipboard. It had a night light attached and a piece of paper with a list of math problems.

"What is this?"

"It's bowling. And it's the SAT."

"I'm sorry, I don't understand."

"Statistics, geometry, functions . . . it's all there. You have your prep test tomorrow. This is your crib sheet."

"I can't cheat, Ronald," I said, with the voice of a hypocrite.

"Of course not," he replied with a kind smile, "but everything we've done the last two weeks exists in what we did tonight. I've reduced it to one sheet. Take a look."

He gunned the Pacer to life while I started to read. It was broken into three sections: Algebra, Geometry, and Numbers Problems.

A ball weighing 6 pounds, moving at a speed of 20 mph will cover 25 miles in how many seconds?

"Listen, I'm going to take Route Nine to the highway, it'll be longer but also smoother," Ronald explained. "It'll take about an hour . . . but that's the amount of time you have to do all those problems. Ready?"

I nodded.

"Go."

I started working feverishly. Every question had to do with bowling. Some made me laugh and some of them made me scratch my head—especially the probability stuff, like calculating the odds of throwing five strikes in a row. Brutal. But when I stumbled, Ronald was there with small helpful hints and tricks to pull the stuff together. He was teaching me a new language I hadn't realized existed.

I finished about five miles from my house, somewhere

near where the old Post Road crosses Goose Hill, and I took the extra time to check over my work. *Gross Rule #23: Always Proof Your Work!* When Ronald stopped in front of my house, I handed him the clipboard and he took out a little red pen and began going over the problems. For him, it was like reading Dr. Seuss—first-grader stuff—and he zoomed over each problem, marking checks for correct answers and annotations on the problems I got wrong. I'd missed a handful, but as I watched him go through the questions, I felt a little high knowing that I was getting a whole bunch right.

"Fantastic," he concluded.

"What did I get?"

"Don't worry about that. It's not about the score. It's the method, your approach, and believing in yourself—and I know you felt you had it—right?"

I nodded.

"You're going to do well tomorrow."

And you know what? I believed him.

"Thanks, Ronald. For these last two weeks. You've been so awesome."

I put my arms around him and gave him a hug—a long hard, squeeze. He held me for a second and laughed nervously. But when we pulled apart, there in the closeness of his car, for the first time, I felt what I can only describe as an energy between us. I couldn't quite believe what I was feeling, but there was part of me that longed for him to kiss me. As if picking up on my vibes, he moved toward me ever so slightly—gentle and tender—but just as we neared . . . the lights on my front porch snapped on and a flashlight poked through the night. It lit us up in the car.

DAD!!

Ronald jerked back, embarrassed.

"Well, um, good luck tomorrow," he blurted, all a-fluster. He quickly started up the Pacer. I leaned over and kissed his cheek—friendlike—and got out of the car.

I smiled to myself—a little confused, a little thrilled— as I walked toward the front door and my father's forthcoming lecture. I had a vision, and it was of Ronald going home and taking out all of his math books and calculating what exists in the moment just before a kiss. He would rack his brains, but I knew in my heart that the answer to that existed only with the poets.

My father was sitting in the kitchen when I entered. He was fuming.

"Late night."

"I was studying with Ronald," I answered. I wasn't even going to get into the whole flashlight thing. A girl has to pick her battles, after all.

"Oh, yeah?"

"We went bowling."

"You went bowling. Before your test tomorrow," he spat. "That's great."

"Yes, but it wasn't about bowling . . . I mean, Ronald broke it down into math."

"I bet."

"Dad, believe me. I learned more about math in the last two hours than I have in the last two years."

He just stared at me.

"You smell like an ashtray."

This fight was for another day, so I turned and walked up the stairs to my room. I was prepared for my dad to say something further, but there was only silence.

I sat on my bed for a few minutes, trying to bring back all the moments of the night. The poetry, the bar, Pete and the motorcycle Ronald fixed, and the test. I lay down on my pillow and looked at the digital clock. It read 11:59. In nine hours, I'd be taking the practice test, and my college career depended on it. At least, that's what my parents and the Terminator were telling me.

I looked out my window, and saw that Ronald's light was on. I closed my eyes and let sleep envelop me.

SURVIVING THE SAT: TIP #5

EXAM DAY

●●●●●●●●●●●●●●●●●●●●●●●●●●●●●●●●●●●

WHAT TO EAT: Your pre-SAT meal is critical for giving you the sustenance to survive this three hour and forty-five minute ordeal. It's best to avoid anything heavy— pancakes, French toast, your mom's super omelets, etc. etc. are all out!—because if you overeat, you will almost undoubtedly slip into a food coma about an hour in. The smart SAT taker will have a bowl of cereal and maybe a piece of fruit a few hours before.

WHAT TO WEAR: Comfy clothing. Period.

WHAT TO BRING: Obviously the basics are essential— picture identification, at least ten pre-sharpened No. 2 pencils, and two non-graphing calculators (in case one goes on the blink). But like the Boy Scouts, this test taker suggests bringing along a few extra things so you're pre-pared for every eventuality:

1. Kleenexes. Whether you're sneezing from allergies, or crying from despair, you gotta get those tears out of

the way so you can see the test. Have a mini-pack in your pocket.

2. Sugar Boost. About three hours in, you might start to fade. Make sure you have some sugar on hand to give you that extra push to the end. I suggest M&M's because, as the saying goes, "They melt in your mouth not in your hand." Plain or peanut is left to your discretion.

3. Earplugs. Yes, the proctors are supposed to keep things silent, but what if the goon behind you is hacking up a lung? Shut distracting noise out with a couple pieces of handy foam. For the $2.50 they'll set you back, it's worth the investment.

4. And finally . . . Something Lucky. If you're religious, bring a cross, a Star of David, or whatever symbol your religious faith uses. If God isn't your thing, then bring a rabbit's foot, a crystal, or a penny you found on the sidewalk. Hey, you never know what might make things go your way, so why not give yourself every edge?

WHEN I WOKE UP the next morning, I felt disoriented. Obviously nothing had actually happened with Ronald, but even sensing that I might be . . . well . . . attracted to someone other than Brad—not counting Orlando Bloom, of course—was incredibly confusing.

Before it became too big a deal in my mind, however, I dismissed it. I told myself that it was just a brief lapse in judgment. Sort of like when you see a dress at the mall that you're really into, and you buy it, only to come across it in your closet the next week and wonder what you'd been thinking. And considering all the stress I was under—the Taker, Jen's investigation, the SAT—it made perfect sense that I was muddled up.

And so, as I drove my mom's car over to school for the

practice test, I popped in the Bach CD that Ronald had lent me, cleared my mind, and prepared myself for the exam ahead.

There are few things more depressing than having to show up at school on a Saturday, so my spirits were less than soaring as I cruised in to the cafeteria where the practice SAT was being held. The room wasn't very full, and it was pretty much a mix of eager overachieving juniors and disgruntled underachieving seniors. Obviously, I fell into the latter category.

Mr. Fellner greeted me at the door as I came in. He was his usual charming self.

"Are we going to turn things around today, Miss Biels?"

Yeah, like I'd tried to bomb last time.

I guess since it was the weekend he figured he didn't need to look teacherly, so instead of his usual suit and tie, he wore a pair of too-tight—and ohmigod, acid-washed—jeans, topped off by a lime-color polo shirt. And were those Tevas on his feet? Sometimes it's painful to see what your teachers actually wear when they're on their own time. Not that I'd expected the Terminator to be a fashion plate, but still.

I gave Fellner a little salute like a fighter pilot ready for takeoff, and he smirked before handing me a practice answer sheet. Evidently, he didn't believe I had much of a chance.

Grabbing a seat by the window, I set my pencils and calculator out on the desk. Even though there were still ten minutes to go, that feeling of tension and nerves that always plagued me during standardized tests began to set in. It's hard to describe it, really—part vertigo, part shortness of breath, part plain panic.

I'm sure many of you've been through it.

I reminded myself that, strictly speaking, I had nothing to worry about. If I crashed and burned on the practice test and didn't get in to Lettich's class, so what? It wouldn't matter. Things presumably were still on track with the Taker, so no matter how I did today, a good score on the real SAT and an admission letter from Princeton were definitely on the horizon.

Nevertheless, I couldn't help but feel like I really wanted to do well. On the SAT, that is. I'd always thought of myself as a good student, and getting such lousy scores had put the zap on my head a little in terms of how I viewed myself. Whether or not I was using the Taker, I wanted to know that Carly Biels had what it took to succeed on her own.

Next thing I knew, Fellner was passing out a booklet with the questions, and students were putting their backpacks under their chairs.

I took a deep breath and closed my eyes.

You can do this, Carly.

You can do it.

Right before I opened my eyes to start the test—and find out if I was simply born to be an SAT loser—I remembered what Ronald told me to do if I started to panic: picture him funking out to George Clinton.

I did—and I laughed out loud.

Fellner shot me a look, but I didn't care. I was ready to go.

"CONGRATULATIONS, SWEETIE!" my mother squealed as I walked in the door.

Yes, ladies and gentlemen, Carly Biels was back in action.

Right after the practice SAT, a bunch of teachers graded the exams and, after thirty stressful minutes sitting in the hallway listening to my iPod, the Terminator called me into his office to tell me my scores. And are you ready for this? I got an 1860! Sure, it was still a long way from the 2400 Club, but getting my scores up 150 points in two weeks? That was huge.

My father got up and gave me a hug. "We all knew you could do it."

"How'd you hear?" I asked, a little confused. I hadn't

called them from the car on the way home, because I'd wanted to surprise them in person. Same held for telling Ronald.

"Mr. Fellner just called to let us know," my father explained. "He was impressed with all the work you—"

"Oh my God, if only you could have seen the look on his face when he saw what my score was," I said, cutting him off.

It was true. Pack of No. 2 pencils? $2.00. Double latte at 'bucks for caffeine infusion? $4.50. Look on the Terminator's face when I pulled my scores out of the gutter? *Priceless.*

"I just wish I'd had a camera! He looked so . . . stricken!"

My father snickered to himself. I knew he wasn't crazy about Mr. Fellner either.

"You see, Carly," my mother began, ultra-cheery, "you can do anything you put your mind to. It's all about believing in the . . ."

And while she went off on the usual parental pep talk about hard work, dedication, and the world being at my fingertips, I started to imagine how I was going to break the fantastic news to Ronald. I decided that I'd look sad at first—like I'd done badly—and right when he started to console me, I'd beam a huge smile and tell him the truth and admit that I'd actually rocked it. Yes!

"And there's some other good news that we have to tell you," my father said.

"You're buying me a car?"

Hey, you never know.

Dad rolled his eyes in mock annoyance. "No-o-o-o, we're not getting you a car," he said. "The good news is that, at the end of our conversation with Mr. Fellner, he told us that he already made a call to Mr. Lettich and . . ."

He did a little drumroll with his palms on the counter-top.

". . . Mr. Lettich is going to let you join his SAT prep course."

"Isn't that terrific?" my mother grinned.

I got into Lettich's course.

Huh.

As you already know, Mr. *Letch* isn't my favorite person in the world—nor any girl's, for that matter—so the news that I'd be spending extended amounts of time with him didn't make want to jump up and down. And why did I really need him or his course? Between Ronald and the Taker, I already had a good tutor and a good score wrapped up.

I guess I didn't look as excited as I should have.

"We *wanted* you to get into Mr. Lettich's course," my mother prompted. "That was why you were working so hard to do well on this practice SAT."

"I know. That's great . . . I guess."

Either missing or ignoring my ambivalence, my father launched right in.

"From everything Mr. Fellner has told us, this course is incredibly intensive. Remember, you only have four weeks until the next SAT, so time is critical. The class meets every day after school from four to eight, so you're going to have to give up *The Mighty Pen* until after the test."

"Give up *The Mighty Pen*?"

"This is about your future, darling," my father continued. "I know it'll be disappointing to miss out—especially because it's your senior year—but you're going to have to make sacrifices if you want to pull this off."

This was sounding worse and worse by the minute. How was it that I'd gone from wanting to celebrate to wanting to barf in less than sixty seconds? But as it turned out, I was only just grasping the full import of what was happening.

"So, if I'm in Lettich's course all the time . . . without any time to write or edit the literary magazine and so on . . . when am I going to study with Ronald?"

"Study with Ronald?" my mother said, confused. "You're not going to study with Ronald anymore."

What?

"From now on you have Mr. Lettich."

Were they serious?

"But Ronald was the one who got my scores up this far," I said, feeling strangely horrified at the idea of not working with him. I tried to make a rational case. "Maybe it would be better if I just kept up with him. Don't they always say, you know, 'Don't switch horses midstream'?"

I hoped using one of Dad's expressions would get him on my side. I was wrong.

"Carly," my father said, "Ronald did a great job getting you this far, and that's wonderful. We're grateful to him, and we should get him something as thanks; maybe a gift certificate to the mall or something. But Mr. Lettich is a *professional*. This is a tremendous opportunity that you've been given, and you're not going to pass it up."

"So what? I'm just gonna kick Ronald to the curb and not study with him anymore?!"

My mother frowned. "'Kick him to the curb'? You studied with one person, and now you're going to be studying with someone better. It's not such a big deal, sweetie. I don't understand why you're getting all emotional about it."

"I'm not getting emotional . . ."

Was I?

". . . I just think it's a lousy thing to do to someone."

My parents looked at each other and had one of those silent conversations that parents have, while I tried to figure out if I was in fact acting emotional, considering the situation. Finally they turned back to me.

"This isn't really up for discussion," my father said, delivering the verdict. "We're going to be paying a lot of money for you to be in this course, and that's where all your energies are going to be focused."

I knew I didn't have a leg to stand on. I stared at the floor.

"We really think this is the best thing for you," my mother said. "Why can't you see it, too?"

For better or worse, I knew that, from every outside perspective, they were right. I shrugged my shoulders in defeat.

As I walked over to Ronald's house to tell him the news, I told myself over and over that there was no reason to be bummed about this. I hadn't wanted to study with him in the first place, so it should be a relief to get off the hook from having to see him all the time. Yes, he was a good teacher, but c'mon, hanging out with Ronald Gross day in and day out? Talking about physics and math? Taking Lettich's course was definitely going to be for the best.

At least, that's what I kept saying to myself.

Before I even got to the front steps, the door opened and Ronald bounded out.

"How'd it go?"

"Pretty good," I answered, not meeting his eyes, with my hands jammed in my back pockets. It only struck me then that Brad had neither called to wish me luck nor checked in to see how it had gone.

"Don't be cagey with the Gross."

"An 1860."

"1860!" he shouted. "CB, that's awesome!"

"It's fine," I answered. A strange guilt—and sadness—swept over me.

"Fine? That's terrific! You're so on your way!"

The happier he was for me, the lousier I felt. I wanted to disappear.

"They gave you the exam back with the questions you got wrong, didn't they?" he asked. "Why don't you get it, and we can go over them right now while it's fresh in your mind. I have an hour before the debate team—"

"I can't, Ronald," I blurted out.

He took a step back.

"All right, that's cool," he said. "We'll do it on Monday night, then."

I looked away—toward the park in the distance—and bit down on my lip.

"Look, Ronald. Since I did so well on the practice test, Fellner hooked me up, and . . . well . . . he got me into Lettich's course."

"Lettich's course?" Ronald squinted. "So what does that mean?"

I took a breath.

"It means I'm not going to be able to study with you anymore."

There. It was out.

Neither one of us said anything, and some old man in a car motored down the street behind us.

"The course meets five days a week," I explained. "And I'd love to keep studying with you, because you've been so great. But Lettich's course is a tremendous opportunity for me. I can't pass it up."

My father's words coming out of my mouth.

"But you're not going to learn anything with him," Ronald said, disappointed. "It's all about tricks, with

Lettich. You're smarter than that. You don't have to be one of his SAT monkeys."

"I just want to do well on the test," I said with frustration. "However I do it."

There was silence again.

"Believe me, Ronald, if I could have it my way, I'd keep working with you, too. But there just isn't going to be time. Between his class, doing my homework, and trying to maintain some semblance of a social life, I just don't see how—"

"I get it," he said. I could tell he was really hurt. A moment later, he glanced at his watch and took a few steps back. "Well, I should get some things organized for my meeting. . . ."

I moved toward him to try to make things right. "Ronald—"

"It's totally fine," he said, putting his hands up like I should stop. "I'm sure it'll go really well for you in Lettich's course. I'll see you around."

And with that, he turned, went back into his house, and shut the door.

I stood there on his lawn, not knowing what to do—feeling like I'd just dumped someone I didn't really want to dump. Soon, the sprinkler system for the house next door kicked on and there was the hushed *chiga-chiga-chiga* as water sprayed across the already leaf-covered grass.

I headed back toward my house with a hollow feeling in my chest. As I crossed the street, I replayed the conversation over in my head, and I tried to figure out if there was a way I could have handled it better. At the end of the equation, though, how I'd told him didn't really matter. All that did matter was that I wasn't going to study with him anymore. I was moving on to someone else.

And much to my surprise, as everything that had just happened settled in on me . . . a tear fell from the corner of my eye.

I brushed it away and kept walking.

But another soon followed.

SAT Vocabulary Builder:

betray

Definition: *v.* 1. to break faith with or fail to meet the hopes of someone 2. to reveal oneself unknowingly or against one's wishes

cold

Definition: *adj.* 1. a temperature much lower than that of the body 2. *slang.* lacking kindness or pity, being harsh

---

I SPENT MOST OF Sunday morning sitting at home feeling depressed. No amount of IM-ing with Molly and Jen, watching MTV, or even working on my short stories could help. From my point of view, it pretty much came down to this:

I was lame.

For starters, I should've made more of a stand with my parents about continuing to study with Ronald. He was a really good tutor—I knew it deep down, even if they didn't—and no matter how good Lettich was for other kids, it was already clear that Ronald could legitimately help me. Worse than the studying part, however, I'd made Ronald feel like what we had done together meant nothing. That he meant nothing. It's a strange logic, I know, since, strictly speaking, he was the one helping *me*, but either way, I'd messed up, and I couldn't figure out how I was going to fix it.

But there was something else that was bothering me. The Taker.

I was starting to have second thoughts.

Maybe I'd become overconfident after having gotten my scores up a hundred and fifty points, but I'd begun to think that perhaps I could do well on the SAT on my own. Sure, I wasn't necessarily about to jump into the 2400 stratosphere, but wouldn't it be better to get, say, a 2100 on my own, than a 2300 with the Taker?

Besides, the guilt was beginning to eat away at me. I

was a cheater. I'd crossed the line from being a good person to a not-so-good person. Some people say it's a weakness of mine—my never wanting to let people down—but I had this nagging feeling that by using the Taker, I was letting down the most important person of all: me.

And at the end of the day, what was doing well on the SAT all about? It was about pleasing my parents and being the person they thought I should be. But would they like me it if they knew what I was doing to get there? Would I like myself when I got there? If I got there? What if I got found out? By Fellner? By the school? By Jen?

I was beginning to doubt that the ends would ever justify the means.

But no matter how I felt about the Taker, I'd started something in motion that I didn't know how to stop.

By now, fall had set in with a vengeance. The woods around Guilford were splashes of reds and oranges, and come Monday morning, the thermometer outside our back door hovered just below forty degrees.

The first real cold snap of the year always perked up my spirits. I loved breaking out my wool sweaters and heavy jackets, and as I made my way through the day of classes, it seemed like the whole school was energized by the crisp weather. Talk of the Homecoming dance, state championships, and Christmas break became the focal point of lunchtime conversations, and remarkably, I was able to temporarily forget about my problems.

During my free period before AP chem, I had a meeting with Mrs. G. about the latest set of stories I'd turned in for my independent study. We chatted for a while before getting down to brass tacks.

"So what'd you think of my pages this week?" I asked.

She smiled and pulled at her earlobe. "Carly, you're a very talented writer. I've always told you that."

"Thanks."

"And the fundamentals here are as strong as ever. The sentence structure, the metaphors, the word choice—it's all rock solid."

You see? It *was* turning out to be a good day.

"So, just take what I'm about to say in context. Don't blow it out of proportion."

Oh.

I started to pull out copies of the stories I'd brought along so I could take notes on her critique, but she motioned for me to stop.

"My thoughts are bigger than what you wrote. It's more a . . . general philosophy of writing that I think would be worthwhile for you to spend some time reflecting on."

I crossed my legs nervously and waited.

"As good as your writing is, I still feel that your stories are missing something very important. Namely, *you*."

"Me?"

"Yes. Your voice."

My *voice*? I'd written them, hadn't I? Wasn't that my voice?

"When a writer is successful—and I'm not talking about making a lot of money, I mean as an artist—it's because she's sharing a part of herself with the reader. Exposing herself. And that means taking risks."

If she only knew the risks I was taking. In real life, that is.

"Riiiiight."

"And so it has to come from a personal place."

Okay, I was lost.

Mrs. G. paused as she formulated her words.

"I guess I get the feeling that you're always writing what you think *I* want. The type of stories you think *I'm* going to respond to—polished and plotted, like Updike or Fitzgerald. But that isn't what you should be doing. If you're going to mature as a writer, you need to write for you and for no one else."

"But I want people to like my stories."

"Of course," she agreed. "But people will like them more if you allow your own style to come through. Don't try to imitate other writers. Do you understand?"

I needed to think about this a little. "I guess so."

She reached out and gave me a pat on the shoulder. "Believe in your own voice a little more—that's what will take your work to the next level."

I smiled and nodded—but to be honest—I still didn't really understand what she was getting at.

Lettich's class was held at one of those drab office parks out in the middle of nowhere, where you pray you never end up working. There was a man-made pond out front that was supposed to make it look all natural and stuff, but truth is, the place was just plain ugly.

I thanked Molly for the ride—what would I do without Molly and her wheels?—and walked in through the swinging glass doors. A bunch of students were hanging out in the hallway, as there were still five minutes before the class began. I recognized some of them from GHS, but others I'd never seen before, and I waited awkwardly for a few minutes until, much to my surprise . . . Jen walked out of the bathroom.

"CB!" she said, with a wave.

"What are you doing here?"

She made a motion with her head for us to move away from the other kids, and we went and sat down in the otherwise deserted lobby.

"I'm just staying for the first half," she explained. "Lettich is letting me sit in on the class for a little, and then he's giving me a interview during the break. I told him I'm doing a profile on the best SAT prep courses."

Jen smirked and gave me a knowing nod. I understood what she was really up to.

"You're smooth," I said. But truth be told, I was getting tired of Jen's obsession with the SAT.

"Did you know that Mr. Lettich used to work for the College Board before he became a teacher?"

"No, I didn't," I answered, and looked out the window. "Go figure."

Whether or not Jen was aware of it, I'd put some distance between us the last couple of weeks. Yes, I still loved her dearly—and I knew we'd always be super close—but I was finding it hard to deal with her relentless investigation of the Taker. For starters, it made me paranoid about getting caught, but putting my involvement aside, it had gotten kind of annoying to listen to her go on and on about it all the time. You know how some girls can only ever talk about their boyfriends? Well, Jen had gotten that way—about the Taker.

"But you want to know what's really cool?" she asked.

I said nothing, and she plowed on.

"I've narrowed down my search even more. Remember when I said there were ten students I was watching? Well, five are here in Lettich's class and four are working with private tutors. But there's one person who's a total anomaly, and that's who I'm completely focused on now." She leaned in close to me. "*Rick Sorenson.*"

"Oh, yeah?" I said, not meeting her eyes.

"I mean, let's get real. He's not studying with any tutor, but I heard he's telling everyone on the lacrosse team that he's got it in the bag."

I, of course, already knew that Rick was a dead end.

"Somehow, I figure that he must have gotten access to someone who—"

I'd been so happy to forget about all of this drama for a day. And now she'd come and ruined it.

I cut her off.

"Jen. I'm glad this is going so well for you, and I'm impressed with all your work, but don't you think you're going a little far with this?"

She sat up straight.

"What do you mean?"

"We used to talk about other things. Classes . . . guys we liked. And now all you're ever interested in is your article."

"But this is a big story," she said, and I could tell she was a little offended. I had the sinking sensation that we were slipping into a fight.

"I know, but there's more to life than the SAT and the people who may or may not be cheating on it. I'm tired of talking about it day in and day out." I paused for a second, trying my best to steer the conversation away from being just about her. "I mean, think about it; what is this whole SAT thing doing to all of us?"

She just looked at me—clearly pissed. Neither one of us said anything for a few moments.

Saving our friendship from further damage, the front door flew open, and Mr. Lettich cruised in and shook his car keys.

"Let's go everyone! Iiiiiiiiiit's showtime!"

Tori Clemens was sitting right behind me, tapping the leg of my chair every so often with tip of her Prada boot.

It was driving me crazy.

"All right, troops," Lettich continued. "This is the time

in the course when we start going over the most critical techniques that'll help you rock the SAT. You ready to bust it?"

There's nothing so lame as adults who think they're cool by whipping out lingo that they've heard teenagers use—usually on TV. It just sounds dumb coming out of their mouths, and inevitably the words are like, two years old.

"But first, I want you all to welcome a new addition to our class." He gestured toward me. "Give it up for Carly Biels!"

When had Lettich started acting like he was trying to get a VJ job on MTV?

A couple of people whooped it up, and I waved bashfully to the rest of the room. I noticed that in her seat in the back, Jen didn't even look at me.

"Okay, okay. Let's get down to business," Lettich said. He put on his glasses, folded his arms, and faced the class.

"I know that a lot of you are good students who've excelled at your respective high schools, but none of that matters now. It doesn't mean shit."

Ugh.

"Everything you've learned from your teachers . . . I want you to forget it."

He put his hands on the table in front of him and pushed his head forward dramatically.

"From now on . . . you're in the Lettich Zone."

And it only got worse from there.

Lettich's point of view—from what I gathered during that first afternoon—was pretty much that he was God's gift to struggling SAT students everywhere. I wouldn't have been surprised if he'd had us bow and swear allegiance. The gist of the course was that, being successful on the SAT wasn't about being smarter than the next person, but knowing how the people at the College Board formulated the questions; being able to see what they were testing you on, and adapting yourself to the problem. The idea of learning for learning's sake was clearly an alien notion here, and it was all about recognizing a type of problem and immediately applying the techniques he was about to teach us. I guess it was a practical method, considering the goal was, after all, to get a good score, but Lettich's mantra and philosophy was on the opposite side of the spectrum from Ronald's. In fact, it looked like the course was about to shape up exactly the way Ronald had described.

"You're not using the method!" Lettich unloaded on one student who had gotten a practice question wrong. "Follow the three steps. One—IDENTIFY: Identify what kind of problem it is—percentage, probability, triangles, etcetera. Two—APPLY: Apply the correct Lettich Technique. Three—SOLVE: Solve the problem and move on to the next question, using the least amount of time possible. Now repeat the three steps to me. . . ."

The hours wore on, painfully slow minute after painfully slow minute, and though I'd filled three pages with notes on how to deduce the right answer for a ratios problem, I couldn't even begin to tell you why the right answer was the right answer. I just applied Lettich Technique Number Seventeen, and *voilà*. Something concerned me, though. Sure, using this approach would be fine if the ratio question on the SAT was exactly like the one he was showing us, but what if it were slightly different? The formula he was teaching us wouldn't necessarily work. Then what?

I raised my hand and asked this very question.

"It won't be different," he answered with confidence. "This is the exact type of ratio problem they'll ask."

"But I've seen other types of ratio questions," I countered carefully, knowing that it's never good to challenge a teacher. "Couldn't they give us one of those?"

For a moment, it looked like Lettich was going to yell at me, but instead there was a visible change in his demeanor and he strolled up to my desk. He put his hand on my shoulder and gave me a squeeze.

"Class, what's the mistake that Carly's making?"

A bunch of people rolled their eyes.

"What's the mistake she's making?" he asked again.

Finally the class droned, zombielike . . .

"THINKING FOR HERSELF."

"Thinking for herself! Exactly!" And Lettich turned back toward me with a grin. "Don't think for yourself, Carly. Your own thoughts are only going to get in the way of the right answer."

Was it just me or was this totally demeaning?

"I know it all sounds a little harsh," Lettich cooed as he rubbed my back, "but all I'm trying to do is help everyone get the best score possible."

"Got it," I answered quickly, so he'd get his hands off me and start feeling up somebody else—like maybe Tori Clemens.

"I realize that perhaps you're a little behind, since you missed the first part of the course," he said. "Why don't you stay after class so I can bring you up to speed?"

Obviously, the idea of staying after class one-on-one with Lettich was right up there with boiling myself in oil, and for the rest of the time I tried to think up an excuse for why I had to leave right away. Unfortunately, I was drawing a total blank. I was supposed to call my dad when the class was over to pick me up, so it wasn't like I could say I was catching a ride with one of the other students. Could I claim a late-night doctor's appointment? Doubtful.

At eight o'clock Lettich finished, and everyone—except me—began packing up their things. Once the room cleared, he waved for me to come closer.

"Take a seat up here at my desk so we don't have to shout to each other."

Shout to each other? It was totally a normal-size classroom. I knew the real reason he wanted me closer.

I moved to the front, and he handed me a bunch of Xeroxes. "These are the handouts that you missed, with sample problems, shortcuts, and exercises."

"Great, thanks."

"And I didn't bring one of the handbooks with me today, but I'll have one for you tomorrow that goes into the whole Lettich Technique in depth. I think you'll find it quite helpful."

"Got it."

I waited for him to tell me more about the course, but he leaned back in his chair and gave me the once-over.

"I can't believe how much you've grown up," he

began. "I remember when you were in my freshman American History class."

I squirmed in my seat. "Yeah, that was a long time ago."

"And now you're nearly heading off to college. Remarkable."

If he'd had a mustache, he surely would've twirled the ends. The man just oozed slimeball. I looked at my watch and sort of tapped my foot like I had somewhere to go, but he made no move to pick up the pace.

"Pretty soon you're going to be an adult," he marveled.

Can I just stop here and ask a question: what's with old guys who hit on teenage girls? It's so . . . disgusting. Do they really think that we're going to be into them, or something? They're just pathetic. Molly told me one time about this director she met who promised to help her get into commercials and stuff, but when she went for her meeting with him at his office, he started acting all weird and smarmy. All he really wanted was to get into her pants!

Lettich pulled his chair up close to mine and opened his pen. "Let's go over some of these handouts."

"Okaaaay."

"You probably don't know this," he said, thumbing

through the papers, "but every year I go through the list of juniors and seniors from Guilford—since I know so many of you already—to look for prospective students. Your name in fact jumped out at me a few months back. I suspected then that you might need some SAT help."

He suspected I might need some SAT help?

Oh, no.

A horrible thought flashed through my head. *What if Lettich was the Taker?* Hadn't he just implied that? And just like breaking down the steps of a SAT problem, the chain of events played out in my mind:

Step #1: Lettich sees my name on the list.

Step #2: He remembers that he thought I was cute (or something equally revolting).

Step #3: Guessing that I might have done badly on the SAT, he takes a shot in the dark and sends me the text message.

Step #4: Foolishly, I take him up on his offer.

Step #5: Being *Mister SAT*, Lettich easily aces the exam for me, OR, since he used to work at the College Board, he has a connection on the inside that's simply going to change my scores in the computer or whatever.

Step #6: I get the good scores back and then have to do

whatever he demands (and knowing Lettich, it isn't hard to figure out what that's going to be).

The idea of Lettich being the Taker—and the nausea it induced—started to make me dizzy. What had I gotten myself into? By now he'd laid his arm across the back of my chair and was close enough that I could smell the gross powdery soap he apparently used. No lie—I thought I was going to faint.

But right then, I heard a familiar voice.

"Sorry to interrupt, but . . . uh . . . are you guys going to be long?"

I looked up and couldn't believe my eyes.

It was Brad. Brad to the rescue.

If Carly had been left alone with Lettich for two more minutes,

    (A) she would've hurled on his shoes

    (B) he would've copped a feel of her boob

    (C) she would've kicked his ass like the chick in *Alias*

    (D) they would've become best friends

    (E) he would've finally revealed himself as the Taker

"YOU'RE SO MY HERO!"

Brad seemed amused by it all and kept driving. "I just figured you'd need a ride home," he explained. "Practice ran long, so I decided to swing by and see if you were still there."

"You're the best." I leaned over and gave him a peck on the cheek.

As soon as Brad had showed up, Lettich backed off

229

and switched into professional teacher mode. What would've taken thirty minutes otherwise, was over in about sixty seconds, and within moments I was out of there. Now that I was in Brad's Explorer going home, I slumped back into the seat and closed my eyes—finally feeling safe again.

"How'd you know where Lettich's class was held?"

"Tori told me."

Tori-friggin-Clemens. Since when had she and *my* boyfriend gotten so buddy-buddy? But I stomped down the part of me that was irked by their friendship. Brad had come to pick me up after all, right? I told myself that my jealousy—or whatever you wanted to call it—was ridiculous.

Brad talked about lacrosse for a bit—about some kid at another school who'd been busted because they found steroids in his locker—but as he talked on, my mind drifted back to what had happened with Jen. Had I been in the wrong to tell her that I didn't want to talk about her investigation all the time? I knew that journalism was super important to her—'cause of her dad and all—but wasn't it fair to take my own feelings into consideration once in a while?

But what I'd asked her rhetorically was actually a legit-imate question: what *was* the SAT doing to all of us? Jen had turned into an obsessive, I'd turned into a liar. The only person who seemed to be surviving the process unscathed was Molly, and that was because she'd totally bailed on the SAT.

As Brad drove on, I started to feel depressed. Was this the first hint of what adulthood was going to be like?

"Where's your bracelet?" Brad asked.

"Bracelet?"

"You know—the charm bracelet I gave you that you always used to wear."

My chest tightened as I remembered that I'd given it to the Taker.

"Oh, the clasp broke," I lied. "My dad's getting it fixed for me."

Brad grunted—seeming to buy it—and nodded. "Listen, I feel bad that I've been kind of . . . you know . . . distant lately," he began. "I've just been really stressed."

"Stressed? About what?" He'd done great on the SAT.

"Oh, you know—lacrosse season, college applications and stuff."

"But you're a total shoo-in at Princeton," I said, placing a reassuring hand on his shoulder.

"I guess," he answered. "But whatever. It's just that I was thinking today that we haven't hung out much the last few weeks. And I want to make it up to you."

We turned onto my street and pulled up in front of my house.

"I've been really busy, too, Brad. It's not your fault."

"Tell you what," he said, taking my hand in his. "Let me take you out on Friday. We'll do a real date—like we used to. We'll do something special."

I smiled. "That'd be great."

"Whatever you want to do. I leave it up to you."

I leaned over and gave him a big kiss. My feelings that things might be amiss with Brad had clearly been wrong.

"Sounds terrific."

Right before I opened the door, a thought sprang to mind. I rummaged through my bag until I found my copy of "Heart" from Young Poets Night. I folded it carefully and handed it to him.

Brad glanced at the paper, confused. "What is it?"

"It's my poem from the other week. A little piece of me . . . for you."

"Neat," he said with a nod. "I'll check it out."

I got out, and as he drove away, he rolled down the window and gave a wave. In turn I blew him a kiss back.

But before I turned up the path that led to my front door—and almost unconsciously—I glanced across the street toward Ronald's window.

The lights were off.

At three A.M., I jerked awake from a horrible nightmare. Drenched in sweat, I staggered to the bathroom and washed my face—desperate to make the hazy recollection of images go away. You know how sometimes when you wake up from a really vivid dream and you can't figure out what's imaginary and what's reality? Well, that's what this was like. And it was terrifying.

In my nightmare I was back in the parking lot at the mall. It was in the future—after the SAT—and as agreed, the Taker had gotten me the score he'd promised, and now it was time for payback. As I got out of the car, I stared into the shadows—underneath the pillar where he'd been last time—but as I got closer and closer to the darkness, I realized that he wasn't there. Relief and joy flooded through me as I figured that he'd decided not to collect on whatever was owed to him. But right as I was about to turn to go back to my car, a gloved hand clamped down over my mouth from behind, and I heard his voice, hot and damp in my ear.

"So good to see you, Carly."

Releasing his hand from my mouth, he took me by the shoulders, and slowly—like in super slo-mo in the movies—he turned me around to face him. At first I couldn't see who it was beneath the wide-brimmed hat, but when he lifted his head and the fluorescent light shone down from above, I saw his face. It was Lettich!! Just as I'd feared. I tried to scream, but when I opened my mouth, nothing came out, not even the tiniest of squeaks. I tried screaming again, but once again nothing happened. I had no voice. With tears now streaming down my face, Lettich laughed a sickening laugh, took off his glove, and laid it on my cheek.

That's when I woke up.

Even after ten minutes of talking myself down from the nightmare, I was too scared to go back to sleep. I've never been a big believer in dreams portending anything in the future, but I was beyond freaked. Worse than my racing heart, however, was my realization that there was no one I could to talk to about it. About the Taker. I was totally alone. I couldn't tell Jen, because she'd expose me. I couldn't tell Brad, because he'd think I was pathetic and dump me. And I couldn't tell my parents, because they'd be devastated, and yet again I would've let them down. The only person in that dark moment who seemed like he could be my confidant was fifty yards away in the house across the street—but I'd blown it with him.

I lay back in bed and pulled the covers up tight around my neck—eyes wide open—and waited for dawn.

SAT Vocabulary Builder:

twit
Definition: 1. *n.* a silly or annoying person 2. *n.* fool

acumen
Definition: *n.* keenness of discernment or judgment (Which I clearly have been lacking lately.)

IF THERE WAS ONE glimmer of hope on the horizon—it was my date with Brad. All week long I was looking forward to it. So when Brad called me Friday night to announce that Rick and Tori the-bitch Clemens were coming out with us, I was devastated. First of all, when had

Tori started hanging out with Rick? Second, Brad knew how much I disliked her and her snobby clique. And as for Rick Sorenson, well I don't need to tell you how I felt about him. That said, it was a Friday night, and after having studied for regular classes and crammed Lettich's course every day, I was ready to let off a little steam.

When Brad pulled up, I was sitting on the front porch, wearing my favorite pair of jeans and a blue shirt with a white tank underneath. My skin had a fading tan from the summer, but I liked to think that I still looked good. I walked to the curb, and Brad got out and gave me a soft peck on the cheek and opened the door for me. Whatever flaws he had, I could never say he wasn't a gentleman when it came to manners. He opened doors and minded his p's and q's.

"So what's on tap for tonight?" Brad asked.

"I don't know," I answered. "I thought you made a plan with Rick."

"No. He just called and said he wanted to tag along with whatever we did, and that Tori was with him. How could I say no. He's a bud. You understand, right?"

"Yeah," I said. But I didn't. "Movies?"

"There's nothing to see."

"True."

"We could just hang at Rick's—his dad is really hands off."

That's all I needed—a night of hands-off parenting. So what—Brad could push me to go all the way while Rick and Tori probably have sex on their first date in the next room?

Nuh-uh.

"No, I've been in studying all week—let's do something different, something wild."

"I like it." He grinned. "What are ya thinking?"

I don't know why I suggested it, but at that moment, it was what I wanted to do most.

"Bowling!"

Brad erupted into laughter. He slapped the steering wheel a few times and then picked up his cell and hit # 1.

Hey, I should be # 1!

"Yo, what up, bro?" he said. "The lady here wants to go bowling—what do you say?"

Brad said a couple uh-huhs before turning back to me.

"Rick says the bowling alley in Branford went out of business, and there's nowhere to go, except Stratford—and that's like an hour away."

"Tell him I know a place in the sticks of North Durham, near Middletown—it'll take forty minutes."

Brad nodded. "Carly knows a place. We'll swing by in about fifteen minutes."

By the time we'd picked up Tori and Rick, I'd realized that I'd stuck my foot in it. Somehow, in a moment of capricious exuberance (note the definite SAT words), I'd convinced Brad and Rick to go to Cody's with me. Even as we passed by the dairy farms of Durham—and Tori blabbed on about some bikini she'd just ordered online—I had a bad feeling in the pit of my stomach. You know what I mean—that butterfly feeling you get after you've made a decision that is just flat-out wrong? I'd been making too many of those kinds of decisions lately.

"Maybe we shouldn't go to this place," I threw out, in an effort to backtrack. "It's a little weird inside."

"Car-Bear! Don't go south on us now!" said Tori.

"Carly's no quitter." Brad intoned as he gave my cheek a playful pinch.

"I'm just warning you guys—this place has some funky characters. A lot of rednecks and bikers."

"Rednecks, cool," Rick grunted. "So how do you know about this place?"

Without thinking, I told them the truth. "Ronald took me here a couple of weeks ago—to show me how probabilities work. It was really helpful."

I knew I'd made a mistake before the first word left my lips. I could feel the heat of Brad's eyes on the side of my face, and there was an odd silence that filled the car. I guess I should've made something up.

"Probabilities with Ronald Gross," said Rick. "Um, Carly, what's the probability that that little nerd has a crush on you?"

"I'd say . . . one hundred percent," Tori chimed.

"Enough," Brad said. "He's helping her. I'm cool with that even if he likes her." He put his hand on my back and pulled me over to him. It was one of those unexpected Brad gestures that reminded me why we'd been together as long as we had.

With my head resting on his shoulder, I spotted what looked like my copy of "Heart" sitting in Brad's console.

"Did you read my poem?" I whispered.

"Yeah, I did," he answered. "I'm not Joe Poet, but it seemed all right."

All right? I looked at the paper again—the way it was still folded so neatly—and I could tell he hadn't even opened it.

"Someone actually called it Plathian," I said.

"Plathian? I don't get it."

"As in Sylvia Plath . . . the poet."

By now Rick and Tori had dialed in on our conversation.

"Who's Sylvia Pat?" Rick asked as he leaned forward between the seats.

Brad pushed him back before rubbing his temples. "Plath. Plath. Isn't she that crazy chick writer who offed herself?"

I shifted back toward my window. I was more than a little disappointed. "Yeah. Exactly."

When we pulled into Cody's, the place was hopping, and we piled out of Brad's truck and headed toward the entrance. The usual crowd of beer-guzzling bikers was hanging outside.

"Get a load of these losers," Rick said under his breath.

Tori edged closer to Brad. "It's like the missing link convention."

But as we passed the crew of bikers, I couldn't miss how the smell of disgust hung in the air. That is, *their* disgust with us. It was a far cry from the reception I'd received when I was with Ronald. Then again, Ronald hadn't been wearing a tie-dyed *Guilford Lacrosse* shirt.

Once inside, I breezed ahead of the group and

headed right for the front counter. Old Leather Pants was manning the ship, and I smiled, hoping she would remember me.

"Hi!"

She took one look at Brad, Rick, and Tori filing in behind me—and smirked.

"Sorry, no lanes."

Brad and I gazed out across the bowling alley. There were a bunch of free ones at the far end.

"Fifty-four looks pretty empty to me," Brad tried.

"Being repaired," she shot back. Cody looked back at me and then asked the question I didn't want to be asked. "Where's Ronald?"

Out of the corner of my eye, I saw Brad stiffen. "Uh, we're only studying partners."

"What?"

"I mean, this is Brad. Brad's my boyfriend. He's on the lacrosse team."

Lacrosse team? That's the best I could do?

"Save it for somebody that cares," Cody snorted. "No lanes."

"But we drove all the way from Guilford," Tori whined.

"Yeah, lady," Rick seconded.

Cody glared at me, and I forced a smile.

Just then a hillbilly-looking type and his wife jiggled up to the counter and dropped their shoes on the desk. "We're done. Thanks."

"Perfect!" Rick cheered.

Obviously pissed, Cody grabbed the shoes off the counter and—without even spraying them with whatever they spray shoes in bowling alleys with—slammed them down in front of us.

"Lane forty-six!"

"But these aren't our size," Tori protested.

"Bowl in your socks then . . . Or if you don't like it, leave!" She snatched the shoes away and turned around, heading into her tiny back office.

"What a bitch!" Rick huffed.

"For real."

We walked over to lane forty-six and took off our shoes. By this point I was already miserable and regretted having brought them here. The guys started skating around in their socks—acting like total jackasses—and more than a handful of regulars at the adjoining lanes gave them the hairy eyeball. Happy to get some distance from my companions, I went off with Tori in search of balls.

"So how are things with Brad?" Tori asked.

"Good. Really good."

"Brad tells me that you're spending a lot of time studying for the SAT. That can be—like—really brutal on a relationship," she said, like she really gave a shit.

"Actually, everything's just fine." I bristled. Shifting subjects I asked, "So are you and Rick an item?"

"Rick? No!" she said with a girlie laugh. "We just hang out sometimes."

"Oh."

"I think he's hilarious."

Rick Sorenson, hilarious? Was I missing something?

We found four balls that were suitable, and being the ultra-considerate person she naturally was, Tori carried hers off and stuck me with the other three. I stood there, trying to figure out how I was going to manage them all, until I looked up toward our lane to see if Brad would notice me and come over and give me a hand. Too busy making fun of some overweight girls a few lanes over, he was oblivious to my plight. But the more I watched Brad and Rick horsing around, and Tori acting like some kind of prima donna, the more horrified I was that I was here with these people. These were my friends? What did that say about me? And wouldn't Ronald have been totally mortified to know that I'd brought them here? I knew then that I'd betrayed something sacred.

I decided that I'd better just get on with it, so I piled the balls in my arms. I had one in each hand, with the third balanced on top of the other two, and I was actually managing the steps down to the lane, when a booming voice stopped me dead in my tracks.

"Hey, little lady."

It was Pete.

"Hi."

"Where's Ronald?"

"I'm not here with Ronald, Pete, we're only studying partners."

"Why?" he asked bluntly.

"I'm here with Brad . . . He's on the lacrosse team." (Why I kept saying that, I have no idea!)

Pete looked over at lane forty-six—where Brad and Rick were now wrestling like second graders—and shook his head. "Looks like a step down to me, little lady."

I looked down, embarrassed. I didn't know what to say, because he was right. It sure did seem like a step down. I just stood there, burdened by bowling balls that I suddenly no longer wanted to throw.

"Let me help you with those," Pete offered, and he scooped up two of the balls, which somehow fit into one of his hands. He then guided me over to our lane and dropped the balls on the conveyor.

But like a klutz, when I went to put my ball on the conveyor, I slipped and dropped the ball on my big toe. I let out a little cry in pain. Brad spun around—took a look at Pete next to me—and puffed up, misreading the situation. Brad was big, of course—six foot two, one hundred and ninety pounds, and all muscle—and for most people that would be pretty intimidating. But Pete was the size of a house.

"Is there a problem here?" Brad breathed, grabbing my hand.

Pete just stared at us both for what seemed like an eternity.

"Son, you let me know if there's a problem."

Brad sized up Pete and then turned to Rick for backup. Rick—who was as white as a sheet—shook his head slightly, as if to say, "No way, dude—you have to be out of your mind."

"Brad, this is Pete," I said through my sniffles, trying to diffuse things. "He's a friend . . . a friend of Ronald's."

"Oh."

Brad gave me a little glare that I took to be his annoyance that all roads seemed to lead back to Ronald Gross.

"I'm Brad," he said, holding out his hand.

Gracious at first, Pete took it, but then he gritted his teeth and gave Brad's hand a squeeze. A *big* squeeze. Brad winced.

"Boy," he began low, "you ever threaten me again in my house and I'm going to snap this little twig you call a hand in two." Still gripping Brad's hand in his human vise, Pete turned to some folks in the next lane over and said something ominous along the lines of—"Can you play lacrosse with one hand?"

Everyone laughed, and Pete redirected his stare at Brad, who was now whiter than Rick and writhing under the pressure on his hand. But just then—and as if the world hadn't already fallen on my head—Ronald appeared.

"Pete, Cody said you were looking for me," Ronald announced without even a glance my way.

"You know these clowns, Ronbo?" Pete asked with a snarl. "Twiggy here was about to get in my face a moment ago."

"Brad's cool . . . let it go, Pete. He's with me."

A beat later, Pete released Brad's hand.

"All right then, good night to you, little lady. *Boys*."

Pete walked off and got a few gratuitous fist bumps from the peanut gallery on lane forty-five. Ronald turned to Brad. "You okay?"

"Yeah."

"You know that beast?" Rick questioned, pointing toward Pete as he sauntered back to his own lane.

Ronald nodded, but he still didn't turn my way. He may have bailed Brad out, but I knew he was furious that I'd brought this trio of clowns to a place that was special to him. And as silently as Ronald arrived, he also departed, disappearing back into the crowd by the bar.

By my side, Brad was shaking his hand—I suppose trying to take the sting out of it—and he fixed me with a look filled with so much hate, I didn't know what to do.

"Let's go," he said.

"What?" Rick complained. "Dude, we just got here!"

"*Dude*, I'm leaving. You want to stay—get a ride with Gross."

Brad stood up, grabbed my hand, and stalked toward the door, pulling me along. To be honest, I didn't put up much resistance, because I wanted out as bad as Brad did. This night had had so much promise, but then it fell apart: it went from Brad and me alone, to a double date with Tori and Rick, to a near career-ending handshake, to Ronald discovering me there.

It had been a colossal failure. On every level.

* * *

We got into Brad's car and drove in total silence for forty-five minutes. I knew he was angry, but frankly, so was I. Angry that he'd invited Rick and Tori, and angry about how he'd behaved at Cody's. After we dropped off our double-daters, Brad parked at the Guilford Green—a location that was equidistant from both of our houses—and I braced myself for the fight to end all fights. I'd never felt more distant from Brad than in those moments, and there was just a black hole where my heart was.

After a minute of listening to the engine as it pinged cooling, Brad turned my way and stared at me for a long time. I didn't say anything. Like some knight in an ancient battle, I'd decided to wait for Brad to strike the first blow. Defense—my dad always told me—was the best offense.

"Come here," Brad said.

Gently he put his hand behind my head and moved in, giving me a long, slow kiss.

Okay, that wasn't the first blow I'd expected.

"I'm sorry I got so angry before," he said.

"We shouldn't have gone bowling there. It was a stupid idea."

"No, it was cool. I overreacted."

Brad put his arms around me again and laid another kiss on me, longer than the last, and with some added groping.

"Don't you think we should talk about it?" I asked.

"Let's just forget it," he coaxed, and then pulled me close again.

By now, I was starting to get a little suspicious. While I was prepared for a shouting match, Brad was there seducing me with sugar. I decided to play it out before calling him out on it. I wanted to know what he was after that was more important than our relationship.

"My parents aren't home," he whispered.

Bingo!

"Really," I said.

"I thought maybe we could spend some alone time together. . . . I love you, Carly. I want to be closer."

Let me clue you in if you have never been on the receiving end of bullshit this good (and to the guys: a warning that we see right through it). This game begins with the unexpected kiss, quickly followed by the never-again-to-be-heard apology, and then topped off with the L word. But I was having none of it.

"I don't think so, Brad. It's already eleven o'clock and I have to be home by eleven-thirty."

"Come on, Carly," he pressed. "This could be our night."

"Be our night?" I said, barely able to hide my resentment. "Why tonight, exactly?"

"I knew you'd ruin this moment!"

"Ruin it? You didn't speak to me for forty-five minutes, then you kiss me like nothing's wrong, say you love me, and boom! there's a moment? I don't think so, Brad."

"Just forget it, Carly," he said, his face red with anger. "This isn't about a special moment. You're never going to give it up."

Give it up? How romantic. *Not!*

"I don't think that's fair, Brad."

"Why can't you just be like other girls?"

By now I was pretty upset. How could he have even considered bringing sex up tonight?

"Take me home, Brad. Right now."

He punched the dash and started his car.

When we got to my house, Brad pulled up to the curb and didn't even look at me. He just kept staring straight ahead, mute. I jerked my door open, got out, and slammed it shut. I didn't even turn around as his car peeled off.

What an ass.

I walked in, and the lights were out, but I was able to make my way to the kitchen. Seething in rage, I was about to storm the freezer for a pint of ice cream, when something made me pause. The tiny light above the windowsill was on, and sitting on the table . . . was a card from Dad and a present beneath it.

Now what else could a girl want after a night like this, but a little I Love You present from her dad?

I opened the card.

I KNOW YOU CAN DO IT!
-LOVE, DAD

Smiling to myself, I tore open the wrapping and discovered a box in the most beautiful color on earth—Tiffany's blue! Maybe things were looking up. I caught my breath, shimmied the box open, and pulled out the tissue paper, imagining some engraved stationery—or maybe a necklace! But there, underneath all the packaging, was the only present that could properly end that suckiest of nights. It was a book. *The Idiot's Guide to the SAT.*

I wanted to scream. I wanted to walk into my parents' room and wake up my dad and shout in his ear: *You're the idiot, not me!* Instead, I did what I do best. I wrote. I went to the pen drawer, pulled out a big fat black Magic Marker, and wrote my own card:

To Dad, I know you can do it!
-Love Always, Carly

Then I crossed out *the SAT* on the cover of the book and wrote *Parenting* in their place. I put the book back in the box, strung the ribbon around it, and went to my bedroom.

By then, I was too worked up to go to sleep. Switching on the light above my desk, I pulled out my diary and began to write down all the ways in which my relationship with Brad had fallen apart, trying desperately to make sense of it all. And the more I wrote, the more upset I became. But it wasn't just about Brad. All the anxiety about the Taker (or Lettich) and the SAT that I'd been staving off the whole week in anticipation of my date with Brad, now returned with a vengeance. When I came to, I discovered I was just writing one word over and over: *Help—Help—Help.*

I lifted my pen from the page, and for a moment, I truly thought I might crack. You know . . . like, totally lose it? Somehow I kept it together, though, and right before I climbed into bed, I sent a Mayday to the world. I woke up my computer and e-mailed Molly:

Help. I think my life is coming 2 an end. CB

Because it certainly felt that way.

Black Friday.

THOSE WERE THE LAST words I wrote in my diary before
going to sleep.

When I woke up the next morning, all I could think
about was how I'd made a complete and total disaster out
of my life. I walked into the kitchen, and my dad—who
had been sitting at the breakfast table—stood up and
walked out without a word. *Great.* My little return gift had
had the precise effect I'd hope for at the time . . . but
now I regretted it. Dad was pissed, and when he was pissed,
he stopped talking. And when he stopped talking, I felt
guilty. It was an impressive technique that I needed to
master.

I opened the fridge. It was empty: no waffles, no bagels, not even a half-empty carton of orange juice. I looked in the cupboards and found the last serving of mom's all-bran cereal. As far as I'm concerned, all-bran cereal is way-nast, but I was starving, so I poured myself a bowl and began munching away. Each mouthful took about twenty chews, followed by a gag-preceded swallow. Could my life get any lamer?

The doorbell rang and I looked at the clock above the stove. 7:30 A.M. Was my dad going golfing today?

"Dad, are you gonna get that?"

No response.

"Mom!"

No response.

I got up and dumped my bowl of bran into the sink and wiped my mouth with my T-shirt (sorry, Mom, but truth is the bedrock of good writing). The doorbell rang again. And then again.

"I'm coming!" I shouted.

I hustled to the door and swung it open, half expecting to see Ronald Gross with a No. 2 pencil in his chest and the Taker covered with blood behind him.

"Surprise!!"

It was Molly and Jen.

"Um, guys, it's 7:30 on a Saturday—did I miss something?"

Molly and Jen looked at each other and started to giggle. Molly took out her tiny little Kelly bag and pulled out an envelope. It had my name written on it in beautiful calligraphy.

"For me?"

"Oui." Jen nodded.

I opened the envelope and pulled out a small orange card that had a drawing of a man in an old-fashioned prison outfit with horizontal black stripes. GET OUT OF JAIL FREE was printed across the top.

"Monopoly?"

"I didn't have time for something more elaborate," Jen said.

"And this is for . . . ?"

"It provides you with a one-day furlough from SAT prison," Molly explained.

"Very funny, but I can't. I'm studying all day today."

"Seriously, Carly . . . you need to take a day off. And that's what we're here for."

I thought about the SAT and my dad and Princeton. And then I thought how wound up I was over this whole thing and the date last night with Brad. I did need a day off. Strike that: I *deserved* a day off.

"Okay, but where are we going?"

"That's a surprise!" they both screamed.

They say that good friends are always there when you need them. Cliché? You betcha. But like every good cliché . . . oh so true.

Greenfield Stables. Sound familiar? Maybe not; but if you're a girl living in the United States, I'm certain you have your own version of Greenfield. When Molly, Jen, and I were in middle school, there was one thing that bound us together more than anything else. It was our one true love: horses.

Now, when you're seventeen, and you've come to realize that cars are faster than horses, and boys are way cuter, a horse crush is for horsedorks only. I mean, if you're beyond puberty and you still have pictures of horses in your room, you should probably see a doctor—or else you'd better be the best damn jumper in the state. That said, when Molly and Jen pulled into Greenfield, a huge smile crossed my face. It was just what I needed. A little trip back to a place and time when things were carefree, and the biggest exam I faced was the weekly spelling test.

I jumped out of the car and ran to the stables. For a

few minutes the three of us just watched as the horses played inside the training ring, and I immediately eyed the horse I wanted to ride that day. She was a beautiful black mare with a white star on her head. Sure she was on the small side, but she could turn like a cat, and you could tell just by looking at her that she wanted to be free to run. One of the hands told me her name—appropriately enough—was Star.

We all got our horses and took off down the Black trail, which was a single-lane path that was very tight and controlled for several miles and then opened up onto a river ride that was long, smooth, and wide; it was the ideal trail for opening a horse up and finding out what she was made of. When we reached the river, I gave Star some rein, and she took her chance. With her running hard and fast beneath me, the wind blew through my hair, and for a minute or two I left the decaying world behind me, forgetting about Brad, the SAT, and most of all, the Taker.

It had occurred to me on the ride up that the decision to hire the Taker, to take the easy way out of a tough situation, was at the root of every problem I had. It had all begun with him, with the tempting fruit he'd offered me. When I'd crossed that line and signed up with him—and gave up on myself, really—it had sparked all the chaos that had followed. That seed of dishonesty had seeped its way into my life and poisoned every relationship I had.

We dismounted near the top of the hill so the horses could drink some water from a stream that sprang out of a large, mossy rock formation. Molly took the chance to run off into the bushes to pee, and Jen and I stood alone for a few minutes with our three mounts.

"I feel bad that we haven't spoken much the last few weeks," Jen began.

"Me, too."

"I guess I didn't realize how much the SAT was affecting you," she said. "It was wrong of me to blab on about the Taker so much. I'm sure it didn't help things."

"You were just being you. It was me who'd changed."

She cocked her head. "How so?"

"Oh, you know," I dodged. "It all just got me freaked. But I'm better now . . . better 'cause of you guys."

"We've been worried about you!"

I slung my arm over her shoulder. "I can't tell you how much it means to me that you guys did this. I don't know what I would do without you."

"You don't have to worry about that."

But isn't that how true friends are? Even if you don't speak to them for a few days—or in this case a few weeks—

you can pick up right where you left off. I realized then how lucky I was to have Jen and Molly in my life.

I put out my hand—slipping back to middle school. "Pinkie swear?"

"Pinkie swear."

When we left Greenfield at the end of the day, I felt good. I was far from perfect, of course, but I'd definitely left something unhealthy on that river trail. Nevertheless, there was more work to be done. I still needed to talk to somebody about the Taker—a confessor: someone who could give me advice about what to do.

After we dropped Jen off, I asked Molly to swing by Gordy's, a small little diner in central Guilford, where Stepstone Hill and Nut Plains Road meet. We sat down and ordered a couple of cheeseburgers and fries. I was in the midst of trying to figure out a way to tell her about the Taker, when she did what true friends do: she read my mind.

"Cars, what's going on with you?"

"What?" I said.

"I know you say it's the SAT, but I'm feeling something more."

This was it, my chance.

"Can you keep a secret?"

"Oh my God, you're having a thing with Ronald! I knew it."

"What, are you crazy?" I shouted.

"You doth protest too much!" Molly said in a faux English accent—what I took to be her version of Shakespearean acting.

"I think he hates my guts at the moment, but that's another matter." I leaned in close across the table. "I hired somebody to help me on the SAT."

Her eyes went wide. "What—you mean Ronald?"

"No." Then I took a deep breath and let it out. "About a month ago, the day we all got our SAT scores and I bombed, I got a text message. Somehow this guy got my number and sent me a message that said 'I can help you . . . the Taker.'"

"And?" she said with a look of horror.

"I ignored him, of course, but then the Terminator scared the shit out of me by saying I had to apply to a community college, and so then . . ."

I gave her the blow-by-blow of my history with the Taker. Molly sat there through the lengthy recounting of the whole saga, not judging, simply listening intently. When I finished, she took a French fry from my plate, popped it in her mouth, and chewed thoughtfully.

"And you have no idea who it is?"

"I have my suspicions. . . ." And I almost told her that I thought it was Lettich, but stopped. For the life of me, I don't know why I didn't tell her. "But they're only suspicions."

"Okay, so let me get this straight," she said at last. "You met this random dude in a parking lot, way in the mall, couldn't see his face, and promised him sex if he delivered a perfect score."

"Not exactly—I mean, the sex part—I didn't promise that . . . He just said I'd owe him whatever he asked for."

"Cars, when a guy says you owe him whatever he asks for, he's asking for sex."

I put my face in my hands.

"I know! Moll, what did I get myself into? I'm scared shitless."

She said nothing this time and took a sip of her Diet Coke.

"Here's the bottom line, Cars—one of us has to go to college, and it has to be you, because I'm going to Hollywood. But if you get caught cheating on the SAT . . . it's lights out."

"I know."

"But all that aside," she added, changing her tone,

"even if you knew for sure you *weren't* going to get caught— you don't really want to use the Taker, do you? I never pegged you for doing that sort of thing."

"I panicked."

Molly touched my hand. "Girl, we all do once in a while. But you should cut it off with him. Look at what it's doing to you."

She was telling me what I already knew—what I'd already decided up on that hill—and I nodded.

"But what if he gets mad that I'm backing out? I don't even know if I can get in touch with him."

"How did you get in touch the first time?"

"He told me to send him a bouquet of flowers to his e-mail and he'd get in touch with me. . . ."

"Perfect!" Molly interrupted.

"But it's not that simple. I'm almost too afraid to do it. Afraid about how he's going to react."

She smiled, and I saw a glint sparkle in her eyes. "Let me give you a little acting lesson here. There's a technique us ladies of the stage use called *substitution*."

"Substitution?"

"Yeah. When you have to summon a certain emotion with another actor on stage—whether it's happy, sad, depressed, strong, or whatever—you substitute someone you know better for the person you're playing opposite; that way you give yourself a little extra juice. So when you're writing the Taker and telling him you don't want him in your life anymore, just imagine it's someone you'd have no problem getting rid of. Someone like . . . say . . . Ronald Gross."

I looked down at the table. "I don't think Ronald is a good example."

Molly looked at me quizzically before deciding to stay on the matter at hand. "Then pick someone else. But trust me, Cars, if you do this, you'll have all the strength you need to do what you gotta do. Substitution, my girl."

I think I understood what she was saying.

"Okay."

"And if you need any support—I'm always only ten digits away."

"Thanks," I said with one last whimper. "But don't mention this to anyone, especially Jen. I don't want to be the subject of a Pulitzer Prize–winning expose."

"No worries. You and the Taker, that's safe with me."

When I got home that night, my mom and dad were out on their Saturday night date, and I ran upstairs and turned on my computer. It was now or never. I logged on to my e-mail, wanting to do what had to be done before I lost my nerve.

I saw that there were four e-mails from Brad, but that was going to have to wait. I went on to the net and found the e-flowers site where the Taker had his account. I pulled it up and ordered a dozen tulips and prepared my message.

Dear Mr. T,
Thank you for everything, but I don't need you anymore.
Sorry to end it, but I think it's better this way.
I hope there aren't any hard feelings.
Carly Biels

I put the arrow over SEND, my hands shaking, but couldn't summon the guts to push the button. Remembering my convo with Molly—I racked my mind for someone else to imagine sending the e-mail to. Someone I'd be happy to never hear from again.

And then it hit me. I pressed SEND.

Bye-bye, Tori!

It was one of those moments when the relief was so great that I wanted to get up and dance, but I settled for pumping my fists and letting out a little cry of victory. Sometimes it feels good to do the right thing.

With that resolved, I went back to read Brad's e-mails. The four were lined up right in a row. The first just said, "Baby"; the second, "I'm"; the third, "so"; and the fourth? "sorry." But before I could decide how I was going to respond to Brad's missives of apology, my computer dinged with an incoming message. It was from virtualflorist.com about my order:

This e-mail account takeforme@hotmail.com has been closed. Your flowers and message cannot be delivered.

THE BARRISTA AT 'bucks handed us our double lattes, and Jen and I grabbed two of the comfy chairs by the windows.

"Thanks again for the other day," I said. "I really needed that."

Jen winked and blew across the top of her coffee.

"We've all been going a little overboard lately," she answered. "Sometimes you just gotta unplug from it all."

I grinned and took a bite of my croissant.

I *was* feeling better. Sure, it bothered me that I hadn't been able to end things with the Taker, but in my own mind at least, I believed I was back on the right track. It was only a matter of time until I figured out a way to get in touch with him and call things off, and then the order of the universe would be officially restored.

"So what happened with Brad? Did he call?"

"Oh, he sent me a bunch of e-mails saying how sorry he was."

"And?"

I glanced away. "We'll just see, I guess. With the SAT coming up, I can't really deal with doing a big analysis of our relationship. I figure I'll just leave things status quo and sort it all out later. We've been together so long, you know?"

"Just make sure you stand up for yourself."

I nodded.

Suddenly, her mood changed and she perked up, excited. "I totally meant to tell you, there's a great book I just finished that you should read. I meant to bring it for you, but they probably have a copy of it in the library. It's called *Letters to a Young Poet* by this guy named Rainer Maria Rilke. You should check it out."

"Thanks." I jotted down the title on a paper napkin. "I need to spend more time working on my writing. I've been bad about it lately."

"You've had a lot going on."

"I know. But Mrs. G. always says, 'Writers write'—which I think is true—so I need to get back to it."

Jen tilted her head and nodded, the way she does when she agrees with something. After a beat, her thoughts went elsewhere, and she slid forward onto the edge of her chair.

"Listen, Carly—this is kind of awkward for me—and I know we just spent a day getting away from it, but I need your help."

"Okay, how?"

"It's about my investigation . . ."

Remarkably, I didn't have my usual knee-jerk reaction against the subject. I wasn't exactly thrilled to get into the Taker, but a realization flashed through my mind: if I found out definitively who the Taker was, I'd be able to fire him . . . or end it . . . or whatever you want to call it.

". . . and I promise I'm not getting all psycho about this again—it's just that I think there's a chance that we could make a big break."

"How?"

"Remember when I told you that I was watching Rick Sorenson? Well, yesterday I happened to see him go into the tutoring lab for almost fifteen minutes. He was talking to Ronald Gross."

Ronald. I felt my shoulders go suddenly tense.

"I was hoping you could talk to Ronald and find out what Rick wanted."

I looked away and said nothing.

"I'd ask Ronald myself, but you know him a lot better

than I do," Jen said. "I've said maybe two words to him all year. I just think that he'd be much more likely to talk to you."

"I'm not so sure about that," I breathed low.

"Why? Did something weird happen between the two of you?" she asked, surprised.

"Not exactly," I covered. "I just think that I'm not too high on his list of people."

Jen stared at me, evidently waiting for me to explain what I meant, but I shook my head.

"Never mind. It's too complicated."

I took a beat and thought about what she was asking me to do. I wanted to help her out, but what was I really going to say to Ronald? *Hey there, I know I dropped you like a hot potato a while back, but can you give me the 411 on your convo with Rick?* That didn't seem very plausible.

On the other hand—and you might be surprised by this—there was part of me that was excited about having a reason to talk to him. It would certainly be totally weird at first, but I missed hanging out with Ronald—his quirkiness, his fascination with physics, his goofball humor—and maybe this was as good an excuse as any to get our friendship back on track.

"Don't worry about it," Jen said, patting me on the

knee. "I'll figure out another way. I didn't realize that it would be awkward for—"

"I'll do it."

An in that instant, I saw in my mind how it was all going to work out. Setting things right with Ronald was the next logical step in my return to the Carly that I used to know; the Carly I respected. And the more I thought about it, the more gung ho I was to make it happen.

Jen blinked a few times—as if to make sure she'd heard me correctly.

"When do you need to know this?" I asked, ready for action.

She shrugged her shoulders meekly. "As soon as possible?"

I nodded and saluted.

"Cub reporter Biels reporting for duty."

I FINALLY TRACKED Ronald down on the lunch line leading into the cafeteria. Fortunately there was a pack of girl-starved sophomore guys standing behind him, so with a toss of my hair and a flash of my thousand-watt smile, I was able to cut into line beside him without anyone complaining.

"Hey there," I said.

"The line starts back there," Ronald replied, and motioned over his shoulder.

I winked at the boys behind us. "Oh, I don't think they mind. Do you?"

They shook their heads and said it was fine. *Flawless.* Ronald snorted and rolled his eyes.

"So how's it going?" I asked.

"Fine."

"BTW, you were so right about Lettich's course. He makes you feel like a total robot. Believe it or not, he tells us 'not to think,' because—as he likes to say—'thinking will only get in the way of getting the right answer.' Crazy, right?"

"Well, that's where you wanted to be," Ronald answered, without looking at me.

That was only partially true, but regardless—this wasn't how I wanted the resumption of our friendship to begin.

You see, I'd spent a lot of time thinking about how I was going to approach Ronald again, and I'd decided that simply being upbeat and normal was the best way to go. I reasoned that if I'd been all bashful and apologetic, it would've only made things more tense; like there was some big history we had to overcome. Better just to sweep it under the carpet and try to start afresh. Here's the non-SAT math: friendly chatter + overlooking the past = starting anew.

But this didn't seem to be the right solution.

The line suddenly moved, as the sophomore A-club (the anorexics) ahead of us grabbed their single servings of fat-free yogurt and celery sticks, and soon Ronald and

I were standing in front of the steaming hot table.

"Ah, mystery meat," I said, and gestured toward the gruel that was supposedly shepherd's pie. "Dare we try it?"

He didn't answer, and instead grabbed a peanut butter and jelly sandwich from one of the racks.

"PB and J, eh?" I threw out, feeling foolishly desperate now. "Always a safe bet."

He picked up an apple from the fruit basket and turned on me. "What do you want, Carly?"

His directness threw me, and I felt the boys behind us pull up short.

"Just to talk."

"Talk," he said. "You only talk to me when you want something, so what is it?"

I hadn't counted on so much hostility. Had he really been that hurt? On the other hand, I had taken another guy to Ronald's favorite spot.

"That's not true, Ronald."

"Yeah?" he said.

If I'd had to pick a location for a throw-down, it wouldn't have been in the middle of the cafeteria, in front of like, the whole school. But I was already into the conversation, so I tried to steer us to safer waters. I motioned for us to head over to the always empty—and somewhat obscured—area by the government mandated Food Pyramid and Heimlich Maneuver posters. Grudgingly, he followed.

"I'm sorry we haven't talked," I opened, "but it's like I told you, I've been crazy busy just trying to keep my head above water with school and Lettich's thing."

"But not so busy that you couldn't go bowling at Cody's."

I said nothing. What I felt about that night was too complicated to talk about.

"What do you want?" he asked.

I considered my options, and to be honest . . . I was conflicted. In the interest of our friendship—if that's what I truly wanted—I should've just said: *Nothing, Ronald. I was just saying hey.* But there were other factors in play—other people's futures. Jen was counting on me, after all. I looked away and took a deep breath. Even then, I knew I should've just kept my mouth shut. But I didn't.

"It's about Rick Sorenson."

"Rick Sorenson?" he repeated.

"You know my friend Jen?" He nodded. "She's doing an investigation of people cheating on the SAT and . . . well . . . she's suspicious of Rick. And I guess—I know this is kind of out there but—well, she saw him talking to you in the tutoring lab, and she wanted to know what it was about."

Hearing myself say all this just made me feel ridiculous. When Jen talked about these things they seemed like they could be for real, but now as I repeated it all, it sounded crazy far-fetched. What was I doing? And judging from the way Ronald was looking at me, he obviously thought it was overboard as well.

"As in, was Rick asking me to help him cheat on the SAT?" he asked. "*No*. Rick had a bunch of SAT problems that he wanted me to solve for him. That's it. I said that we'd be happy to work with him on prepping for the SAT, but we don't just hand out answers to practice problems. That's not how the tutoring lab works."

"Got it."

"That's all there was to it."

By this point, Ronald was pissed. He wasn't shouting or anything like that, but he was angry. And his anger had nothing to do with Rick Sorenson.

A wave of regret hit me.

"I appreciate your telling me about it," I said.

"Is there anything else?" he asked.

I looked down at my shoes. There *were* other things I wanted to talk to him about—so many things—but either I couldn't find the words, or I didn't have the nerve to say them in that setting. Either way, when I opened my mouth to speak, nothing came. He waited.

"Hey, Biels!" I heard someone shout. I glanced over my shoulder and saw Brad and a bunch of his lacrosse buddies motioning for me to come sit with them. I turned back to Ronald, still unable to speak.

"The retards are waiting for you," he said.

"Don't be like that, Ronald."

"Be like how?"

"Like *them*."

I'd never said two words I meant more.

He smiled bitterly. "But that's what you want, isn't it?"

I looked down.

He adjusted his backpack and walked past me. "See you around, Carly."

SAT Vocabulary Builder

culpable
Definition: *adj.* meriting or deserving blame or condemnation

dressing-down
Definition: (no, it's not when you wear casual clothes) *n.* a severe reprimand

---

"THAT'S PRETTY HARSH," Molly said. "But I don't really know what to say otherwise."

We were sitting in the offices of *The Guilfordian*, and I'd just finished giving her the instant replay of my meltdown with Ronald, in the hopes that she might be able to give me some insight. After Ronald had stormed off, I'd put on my best game face and had lunch with Brad and his teammates, but deep down I was pretty upset about what had happened. I felt sick to my stomach, and I didn't even eat the chocolate-chip cookies that were served on Thursdays.

"Should I have done something differently?"

Molly twirled her hair in thought.

"I don't know. But it seems to me that there's a more important question . . ." She trailed off, hesitating.

"What?"

"I guess maybe you should ask yourself why it upset you so much."

I leaned back. "Why it upset me? Because I don't want people to feel like I've been mean to them or something. I like to think of myself as a nice person."

Molly rolled her eyes. "Sing that song if you like, but I know you better than that."

My eyes went wide. "Are you saying that I'm bitchy?"

Oh my God! Why did everyone suddenly hate me?

"Relax," she said. "That's not what I mean at all."

"Then what?"

But before I could get into it further, Jen blew in—a wave of papers, words, and energy.

"We're onto something! We're onto something!" she announced as she plunked her bag down on her desk. "Boy, have I got news!"

"What?" Molly and I asked in unison.

Jen looked at me. "You first. Did you talk to Ronald?"

"Ohhhh yeah," Molly joked.

"What?"

"Don't ask," I answered. "But there's nothing really to report about the cheating thing. Rick wanted to know if Ronald would solve some SAT questions that he had."

Jen grinned. "Keep going."

"There's nothing else. Ronald said no."

Jen whipped out her notebook. "You're unbelievable, and this is huge!"

"Huge?" I said, wrinkling my nose. "How?"

"Don't you see? It's clear as day," she said with the utmost confidence. "Rick Sorenson must have a copy of the SAT."

Talk about jumping to conclusions.

"Why else would he need answers?" Jen explained. "Every *practice* SAT has an answer key. Somehow he must've gotten someone to give him a copy of the *real* test ahead of time, and given that Rick's no genius, he'd need to get someone to solve the problems for him."

Molly and I looked at each other. It seemed plausible enough, but still. It was hardly enough evidence to accuse someone.

"Maybe you'd better not get ahead of yourself," Molly cautioned.

"But the plot thickens—there's more!" Jen exclaimed, practically bouncing off the walls. "This is what I was going to tell you guys: I heard—and I can't say from whom, because I gotta protect my sources—that Rick asked Mary Bookman out on a date last week."

My mouth fell open. "As in Mary 'Bookworm' Bookman?"

Jen nodded.

Yes. The plot thickens indeed.

Mary was not . . . shall we say . . . a typically sought-after prize. And she was certainly not the type that anyone could ever imagine Rick being interested in. For better or worse, Mary existed in the outermost orbit of the GHS social galaxy. While I'm sure Mary was nice enough—which could never really be confirmed since she never actually spoke to anyone (or at least anyone I knew)—rumor had it that her mother still made all her clothing for her.

"And why do you think he would do that?" Jen asked.

"'Cause she's a member of the 2400 Club," I answered, getting it now.

"Bull's-eye."

So Rick was approaching all the members of the 2400 Club. Jen's theory was starting to hold some water.

"Have you talked to Mary about this?" Molly asked.

Jen shook her head. "Well, that's where things take another turn. Three days later, he canceled his date with her."

"Which means . . ." I started as I pieced it together, ". . . which means that he must've found someone else who agreed to do it for him in the meantime."

Jen nodded. "Someone else from the 2400 Club."

"You should interview them," Molly said. "You know, the other members—whoever they are."

"Totally. Because maybe one of them will crack and we'll be able to blow this wide open!" Jen smiled. "And I thought we could do it after school, together. The Sistas of Luv; crime-solvers extraordinaire."

Molly scrunched her face, disappointed. "Boo! I can't, I'm sorry. I'm presenting my monologue in acting class tonight."

Jen pouted before turning to me. "Carly? You in?"

If I wanted to get to the bottom of who the Taker

was—once and for all—here was my chance. Yes, I had Lettich's class, but in the grand scheme of things, missing one day wasn't going to break me.

"I'll meet you at three P.M. in the parking lot."

Since Ronald and Mary Bookman were out, a quick glance at Jen's board revealed that there were only two remaining members of the 2400 Club: Yang Ling and Ed Rice. After a brief conversation, Jen and I agreed that Yang Ling was an unlikely suspect. Yes, he was brilliant, but his weak (and that's putting it delicately) grasp of the English language pretty much eliminated him from being helpful to Rick. Yang would've been useless on the verbal section, and strictly speaking, he'd only been an "honorary" member of the 2400 Club because of it.

So that left only one person for us to track down.

"Ed Rice?" the head of the science club said with a squint when Jen and I interrupted their meeting. "No, he dropped out of S.C. in the beginning of the semester. He had to deactivate 'cause he's taking a math course at Yale in the afternoons."

Had it just been me, I would've thrown in the towel and waited to find Ed during, say, homeroom the next day. But when Jen got on the scent of something, there was no stopping her. So this is why—come six o'clock—we found ourselves in New Haven, sitting on the front steps of the math building at Yale.

It was a cool night, and college students clad in fleeces and scarves hurried down the walkways, cradling books and coffee cups. Some walked alone, others in groups, and I couldn't help but begin to imagine what it would be like when *I* got to college. How much fun it would be. Living on my own, the great courses, brilliant professors—the parties! I knew I'd miss the Sistas, but for the first time, the promise of life away from Guilford seemed so close at hand.

Jen had clearly gotten the bug, too, because she'd been silent the last few minutes; a total rarity with her.

"Oh my God. Check out that guy," Jen suddenly whispered. "How cute is he?"

I glanced up the path and saw who she was talking about. He *was* cute. As he passed us—I guess he'd caught us looking at him—he kind of smiled and gave us a wink. We did our best to stifle our guilty giggles.

College. This was it. This was the brass ring. The reason why everybody was so neurotic and crazed about the SAT. I couldn't wait for the day when it wasn't about getting into college anymore—but being there.

Boots thumped down a hallway before the wooden doors of the building where we were sitting swung open. We jumped to our feet and moved off to the side to keep from getting mowed down by the torrent of students pouring down the steps. Jen and I kept our eyes peeled for Ed, but for a good five minutes he was nowhere to be found. It wasn't until the very last of the people left, that Ed emerged—all thirteen years of him—trailing some bookish-looking coed who paid him no attention. He said a wimpy good-bye to her (which wasn't reciprocated), before ambling toward the shuttle stop.

Poor Ed. Like I said before, he was the smartest person I'd ever met—which I guess should be pretty obv, considering he was taking college-level math courses as a high school freshman—but like many a brilliant mind, while he excelled academically, he flailed socially. Oh, he made efforts. He wasn't the nerdy type who had resigned himself to permanent outsiderdom. No, in his one year as a high-schooler, Ed Rice must've asked out half the school, but he was still waiting for his maiden date.

Jen was the first to make a move.

"Ed!"

He jerked his head around—clearly surprised to hear a girl calling his name—and looked really confused when he recognized us. He stopped walking, and we caught up with him.

"Hey, Jen. Carly," he said with an awkward nod and forced cool. "Are you guys taking courses here now, too?"

"No," Jen said with a twinkle—and I saw she was turning on her charm. "We came to see you."

"Oh," he said, pleased. "What do you ladies need?"

I noticed then that he was wearing one of those silk mini-scarves under his dress shirt—you know, like the kind cheesy South American guys wear? It was safe to say that Ed tried a little too hard.

"We wanted to ask you some questions about the SAT," I chimed in, in an effort to keep it casual.

"Shoot."

"Do you do any tutoring?" Jen asked.

"I haven't in the past," he answered, "but I'm sure we could make an arrangement if you think it would be helpful. Perhaps we could do a trade for services rendered?"

"You don't?" Jen pressed—ignoring his obvious play for a date. "I heard that you were working with Rick Sorenson."

Ed looked stricken. "That's not true."

"Really? That's not what people are saying," I said gently, playing the good cop to Jen's bad.

"What people?"

I shrugged my shoulders.

"Why are you lying to us, Ed?" Jen demanded. Even I was taken aback by her guns-blazing approach.

"Uh. Uh." He searched. "I'm not lying. It's the truth."

No one said anything for a few moments. As far as I was aware, Jen didn't know for sure that Rick and Ed were working together—or had even talked, for that matter—but she sure wasn't acting that way.

"We know what Rick Sorenson is up to," Jen said, cold and hard. "And I'm going to break the story wide open in *The Guilfordian*. And either we can do this the easy way—and I'll leave your name out of the article—or we can do this the hard way—and I can almost guarantee you that any hope of your attending a good college will seem like a faint and distant memory."

Wow. It was a radical play on her part, and even I was intimidated. But Ed just stared at her, his eyes squinted tight like some showdown in an old Western movie. All that was missing was some tumbleweed rolling along the walkway.

But then I saw it. It was a twitch of his left hand and a quick look down to his feet. He was crumbling inside.

"Your choice," Jen said. "Let's go, Cars."

"I only did it 'cause Rick said he'd let me hang out with him and the lacrosse guys," he whined as tears began to stream down his cheeks. "He promised . . ." And he trailed off now, beginning to hyperventilate.

Jen stepped toward him and put a motherly hand on his shoulder. "It's going to be okay, Ed, just calm down. If you tell me everything, I'll make sure that you're an anonymous source."

"But . . . but . . ." he blubbered.

"Relax, Ed," I said. And a terrible thought flashed through my head: was this what I would be reduced to if someone found out about me and the Taker? I had to find a way out of this!

Ed managed to get ahold of himself. We sat down on a bench nearby, and Jen took out her reporter's notebook.

"Rick said that all I had to do was solve the problems for him. That no one would find out."

"And you did it?"

He nodded with regret.

"And it was the real test?" Jen asked.

"He said some guy sold it to his dad."

This was huge!

Jen looked up from her notebook—she could barely contain herself. "Did he tell you who sold it to him?"

Ed shook his head.

"Don't hold back on me, Ed," Jen threatened.

"I'd tell you if I knew—I swear!" he cried, and it looked like he was about to start bawling again. I shot Jen a look that she should back off. C'mon, the kid was thirteen.

"And you did this all because you wanted to hang out with Rick and his buddies?" I asked—more like a sister than an interrogator.

"You think it's fun being the alien-smart kid who skipped three grades? Like Doogie-freakin'-Howser?" he cried. "Just for a day—for one day—I wanted to be cool."

"Hanging out with Rick doesn't make you cool."

"That's easy for you to say," Ed shot back. "Try living on the other side."

"That's not true, Ed. We're all on the same side."

Ed's lip curled in disgust. "Oh, yeah? So is that why you're embarrassed to be seen with Ronald Gross?"

How did this suddenly become about me?

"You don't know what you're talking about," I countered.

He didn't answer this time, but let out a guffaw that more than clearly expressed his position.

"Carly's personal life is none of your business." Jen

stepped in. "You have your own problems to worry about."

Ed's momentary aggressiveness disappeared, and he cowered back into his seat. After a moment, he glanced at his watch. "Listen, my mom's picking me up on the corner. Can I go?"

Jen nodded. "But don't come to school tomorrow. This whole thing is gonna crash big, and I don't want that brain of yours to get mashed."

He whimpered, put his hands to his head, and waddled off. Jen just stared down the street after him.

"Harsh," I said.

Jen looked back to me and grinned, triumphant. "Rick Sorenson has had his last laugh."

But if I didn't find a way to end it with the Taker soon, I wouldn't be laughing much longer either.

JEN DROVE BACK to school like a madwoman.

"I have to write this article tonight, before anybody else scoops me!" Jen said, all afire. I glanced over at the speedometer that hovered around fifty-five. We were in a twenty-five mile an hour zone.

"Maybe you better slow down," I suggested. "We don't want to get pulled over."

"You're right, you're right," Jen replied, easing her foot off the pedal. "But don't you see how huge this is? My father would be so proud! Huge!"

It certainly was. So Rick Sorenson *was* cheating on the SAT, and he had a copy of the real exam to boot. But one thing still confused me: if Rick was the Taker, how had he been planning to take the exam for me? Just because he had the test didn't mean that he could get into the exam center, right?

It seemed to me that a big piece of the puzzle was still missing.

"Oh, and don't worry. I'll totally give you credit in the article for your help."

"Don't!" I blurted out, imagining what the Taker—or Rick—might do to me if he knew I had a hand in his downfall. "I mean—you deserve all the credit. It was really your investigation. I wouldn't feel right."

"You sure?"

"Absolutely."

She shrugged her shoulders to say okay, and I breathed a sigh of relief.

As we neared Guilford High, I noticed flashing blue-and-red lights illuminating the surrounding trees, like at a rock concert or something.

"Was there some event at school tonight?" I asked.

"I don't think so."

But it wasn't until we pulled onto campus that we saw what it was: police—everywhere. It was crazy! There were local Guilford police, Connecticut state troopers, and even a bunch of guys with those blue FBI jackets. Something big was going down.

"Holy smokes!" Jen said, and she pulled her Jeep into a space in the senior lot.

We hopped out and started walking toward the front of the building to see what was happening. None of the cops looked too worried—some of them were just standing around talking—so it didn't seem like there was any big immediate danger. Nobody holding anyone hostage, or anything like that. A crowd of Guilford students had gathered behind the yellow police tape that kept anyone from getting too close to the entrance, and they were murmuring in confusion as well.

Soon there was a flurry of squawking on walkie-talkies before the big main doors of school opened, and out came a couple FBI guys escorting . . . Oh my God! . . . Rick Sorenson and his father. In handcuffs! They were being arrested! A couple seconds later, more FBI guys led out . . . I couldn't see who it was at first . . . but at last I did.

It was Tom "the Terminator" Fellner!

Stuff like this doesn't happen in Guilford!

Jen whipped out her digital camera—ever ready for a story—and moved toward the building to get a better angle on the action. I turned to one of the state troopers nearby.

"What happened?"

"Please stand back, young lady," he ordered, and

he motioned for me to move to the side.

I felt someone take me by the elbow. I whipped around. It was Mrs. G.

"Well, now I've seen everything," she said before gesturing for me to come away from the commotion. "Can you believe this?"

"I just got here. What's going on?"

"Rick Sorenson's father bought him a copy of the SAT."

I decided not to let on that Jen and I had just discovered this ourselves. "But why are they arresting Mr. Fellner?"

Mrs. G. smirked. "He was in cahoots with Mr. Lettich."

"Lettich?" I asked.

She pointed toward a state trooper's car parked off to the side. There . . . in the backseat . . . and presumably handcuffed . . . was Mr. Lettich.

"I don't understand? Why'd they arrest *him*?"

"Because he's the one who sold Rick's father the test! Apparently the FBI has had an investigation going on for quite some time—interstate crime or something."

It was all too much to process at once, and my head reeled from trying to make sense of it all. Lettich was the one who sold him the test? But of course. *He used to work at the College Board.* He had a connection on the inside.

"This wasn't the first time," Mrs. G. continued. "Lettich has been helping other students as well."

And then the final piece I'd been searching for clicked into place.

It was Lettich all along.

Lettich was the Taker.

"And Fellner?" I asked.

"From what I've heard, he was receiving kickbacks from Lettich. . . ."

Hence the Porsche, I thought.

"Oh my God, that's crazy."

She nodded. "They think other students are involved."

Oh, no.

Oh, no!

My first instinct was to pull an O.J. and make a run for it. If the FBI had arrested Lettich, then certainly they must've seized his computers or something, right? Isn't that what they always do on those cop shows? And when they searched through his e-mails it would lead them right to yours truly. But if I ran, where would I go? Mexico? On the fifteen bucks I had in my pocket? That was never going to happen.

"I'm sure the FBI is going to want to talk to you," she said.

What?!!

"Me?" I asked, horrified.

"Sure. You were one of Lettich's students after all." But she winked and put a calming hand on my shoulder. "Of course, you have nothing to worry about."

I forced a smile. "Right."

Mrs. G. looked at me with concern. "Carly, you're really pale. Are you feeling okay?"

"Just . . . um . . . so shocked," I mumbled.

She nodded and glanced over at Fellner. He sat in the backseat of one of the police cruisers, his head down.

IT WASN'T UNTIL I walked away from Mrs. G. that the full import of what she'd told me sank in. As I imagined the possibility of being interrogated by the FBI—and exposed for what I'd done—I felt myself starting to crack. See, it was worse than just thinking I was going to start crying. It was more like I felt the whole world was closing in around me, and I was terrified. I took deep breaths in a useless attempt to calm myself.

It's going to be okay, Carly. It's going to be okay.

More than anything, I gradually realized that I just wanted to be home. Safe in the confines of my room, where everything was tangible and my own. Whatever further bad things would happen to me, at least I'd have Mr. Biggles for support. But how was I going to get there? I had

no idea where Jen had gotten to—no doubt deep into inter-
viewing cops for her article—and Molly was still at her acting class. And the idea of calling my parents was more than
I could bear at that point. *Think, Carly, think.* I checked my
watch. It was 6:30. And then it hit me. Brad must be leaving lacrosse practice. I could get a ride from him.

Running across the quad that led to the lacrosse field
and locker rooms, I imagined that a long hug from Brad
might just make it all better. Deep in his arms, I could forget about everything that had just gone down, and maybe
with a reassuring whisper and a gentle kiss on the forehead,
it would all get better.

But it only got worse.

Because, just as I rounded the lacrosse clubhouse, I
caught sight of Brad about fifty yards away, standing under
the bleachers, still in his uniform. But he wasn't alone. He
was standing with Tori Clemens. Standing close. Very
close. They were oblivious to what had been going on in
front of school. They were kind of whispering to each
other and laughing and having a boffo time, and just as I
was about to call out to him, I watched as he leaned toward
her . . . and . . . *NO-FREAKING-WAY* . . . kissed her! And
not kind-of kissed her. *Kissed* her kissed her.

They were making out!!

The urge to throw up spun through me, and if I hadn't lost the power to speak, I surely would've screamed. I even had to grab hold of the side of the building to keep from collapsing as my heart splintered to pieces in my chest. I can't tell you why, but I stood there, unseen for about five minutes, watching them suck face—my worst fears confirmed before my very eyes. Looking back on it, I never knew what "devastated" really meant until that very moment. After a bit, I backed away, feeling too weak to confront them. And what would I say, anyway?

I staggered back to the main building, half dazed, and as I reached the back vestibule, I knew only one thing for certain: my whole life had just come crashing down around me.

I JUST WANTED TO GET HOME.

Desperately.

I ran down toward the south wing—where a few cops were standing around chatting with some FBI agents—and turned right, heading toward the back parking lot, hoping against hope that Jen might still be here. But when I got to the back door and looked outside, her car wasn't there. She was gone. But there was one car I recognized.

Ronald's Pacer.

Of course. He had late tutoring lab on Wednesdays. I took off for the lab at a brisk walk, and as I neared the entrance, the door wasn't open, but I could hear people talking and what sounded like chairs being moved. Strangely, none of the voices sounded like Ronald's. I knocked on the door to announce myself, but nobody responded.

"Hello? Ronald?"

No answer.

I pushed the door open, but when I saw the lab, I froze, aghast. It looked like the place had been hit by a hurricane. Files were splattered all over the floor, desks were toppled over, and wires were scattered everywhere. In the middle of the room, the computers from the lab were piled chest-high on a big cart. Two state troopers who were sorting through everything turned around and looked at me in that who-are-you-and-what-are-you-doing-here way that only policemen can.

"Can we help you?"

"I was looking for Ronald Gross."

"He's in the principal's office, being questioned," one of them answered.

What?!

"Ronald Gross is being questioned? For what?"

But I didn't even wait for an answer. I just turned and ran as fast as I could toward the principal's office. I had to be there for him—to protect him. Maybe it was because of my involvement with the Taker, but I couldn't help but feel that Ronald's being questioned was somehow my fault.

That somehow, by helping me, he'd been drawn in to this huge mess. My heart started pounding through my shirt.

I scaled the steps two at a time, landed on the main floor of the east wing, and sprinted toward the principal's office. It was about two hundred yards, but I covered it in under twenty seconds, simultaneously breaking a world record and arriving at Dr. Meed's office just in time to see Ronald come out. His face was red, and it looked like he was teary-eyed. He took a deep breath and then sniffled.

"Ronald," I called out as I neared.

He looked up, surprised, and his back snapped straight. His hand swiped whatever H_2O remained around his eyes.

"Hey," he said.

In my rush to get there, I'd forgotten that Ronald and I weren't exactly on good terms. He didn't look happy to see me, and I wasn't sure if that was because of the immediate circumstances or the state of our friendship.

"Did they question you?" I asked.

"Yes."

He had an odd look on his face. I could see his brain working right through his skull, calculating thousands of permutations a second. But what he was thinking about, I didn't know.

"I'm sorry. It's my fault."

He shook his head.

"It *is*," I continued. "When I bombed the test—"

"It has nothing to do with you. It was Rick."

I was confused. "Rick?"

"Remember how I told you that Sorenson wanted me to solve those problems for him? Well, what I didn't tell you was that he got pissed and threatened me." Ronald paused. "And now apparently he tried to save himself by implicating me."

"Did they believe you?"

He shrugged his shoulders.

"I'm so sorry, Ronald."

I stepped nearer and put my arms around him and gave him a long hug. Much to my surprise, it was then that he did something a boy has never done with me: he cried in my arms. I'm not sure if it was the echo of Brad and Tori or the pressure of the FBI interview, or the idea that Ronald's future was almost destroyed because of something I was partially involved in, but I let go as well.

After a few moments, we both gathered ourselves and wiped away the tears. Without speaking, we turned and walked out to his car. He rubbed my back a few times, like a big brother might, and I grabbed his hand and gave it a squeeze, wordlessly telling him it was all going to be fine.

On the way home, we drove slowly and without music. When we pulled onto our street I told him to park in his driveway. He didn't ask why—he knew why, I think. He turned the ignition off and we sat there in the dark for a few minutes, not talking.

"Ronald, I was an idiot. I mean, you were the only good thing in my life this past month, and I was afraid . . ."

"Of the SAT?" he said.

I wanted to say more. I wanted to say, if my mind were as honest as my heart, that I was afraid of him, of liking him in a way I wasn't brave enough to live with. Afraid of what Molly and Jen would say, of what Brad would think. Of what the world would do if I walked down the halls of Guilford High with Ronald Gross holding my hand. But all I said was . . .

"Yes."

He smirked. I could tell that Ronald wanted me to say more, too—to lay all the cards out on the table—but he was still the boy across the street who barely dared to speak to me until just a few weeks ago.

"You have nothing to fear," he said. "I know you'll do well."

"How do you know that, Ronald? Because of a practice test? I've blown it before."

"I have to go, Carly. I can't do this anymore."

"I need you, Ronald . . . I need your help," I pleaded.

He opened the door and stepped out. He looked at me for a second and turned toward his house.

"Ronald," I said. But nothing more came out—try as I might to tell him something from my heart.

"The lab is open from three to five on Wednesdays. I'm sure we can find somebody to help you."

"Ronald, I don't want *somebody*, I want you!"

Either he didn't hear me or he chose not to, because he opened the door to his house and disappeared.

I walked into my house and marched straight up to my room, lit a candle, and turned off the lights. I got into bed. I just lay there for hours, staring into that single flame as it flickered. And as the light danced off the ceiling, I began to think about the Taker—or Lettich, I suppose— and Rick Sorenson, and how I'd come within a whisker of blowing my life to bits, all because of a stupid test that told people whether I was good enough for Princeton, or if not, for Penn, or if not, Penn State, and on and on and on.

Why did I care? Why did my dad care so much?

Wasn't it enough to have a bright daughter who went to a good school? That she got a good education?

Not in my world. Probably not in yours either. I couldn't change that—I was going to take that test, but it wasn't going to ruin my life. Whatever the score, I was going to college and I'd be happy wherever I landed. The Taker was gone.

What was going to change was me. Specifically, me and Ronald.

I had to come up with a plan to win him back.

At 6:30 the next morning, I was woken by the sound of my cell phone ringing. It was Molly.

"This better be good," I said.

"Jen's article is on the front page of the *New York Times*!"

I bolted upright in bed.

"Shut up!"

Apparently Jen shared a byline with a metro reporter named John Ryan, and there was a picture of Lettich being led out of his house in handcuffs and a separate picture of the Terminator being led out of the school. According to the article—which Molly now read to me over the phone—Lettich and the Terminator had helped hundreds of students in several states cheat their way into the college of their dreams. Rick Sorenson was named as being their point person to the student body of Guilford HS. No other students were implicated, but the investigation was still going on.

"Are you breathing easier now, Cars?" Molly asked when she was finished reading.

"You mean about the Taker?"

"Ah, duh—it was Rick!"

I didn't tell her that I actually thought it had been Lettich. Well, sort of Lettich, that is. Since Lettich couldn't exactly cruise in and take the SAT for me—it wasn't like he could've passed for a high school student—I figured either he must've had someone on the inside at the College Board to change my scores on the computer, or someone younger on his payroll who would've done the actual test taking. Either way, Lettich had still been my Taker.

"Has Brad heard anything from Rick?" Molly added.

"I wouldn't know . . . Brad and I are over."

"What! How did you not tell me this?"

"It would take too long to explain," I said. "But I actually think it's all a big relief."

Molly was thrown, but she let it go. "Okay, you can tell me all about it when I pick you up."

"To tell you the truth, I was going to call you this

morning. I don't need a ride—I'm taking the bus."

There was a long pause.

"The bus, huh?" Molly said, processing it all. "So is this Ronald related?"

I took a deep breath. "Yes."

"I knew it . . . I knew it . . . I knew it!" She started laughing and then hooting and hollering. It was infectious and I started to laugh as well.

"Am I crazy, Molly?" I said. "Have I lost it or do you sort of see what I see?"

"I totally see what you see—he's a late bloomer, Cars. Two years from now you won't even be in his league. This kid is going to be a firecracker in college. Hook him now while you can, hot stuff."

"Thanks, Moll . . . I'll see you at lunch."

When I got downstairs my dad was sitting down with the paper and his coffee. We hadn't spoken much since the night I'd left him "the present." It wasn't pure silent treatment, but he was less than friendly, and I was less than interested in hashing it out with him at that very moment.

"Your friend Jen is a star," he said with a faint smile as he tossed the paper my way.

"Molly read it to me already. Isn't that insane?"

"Her dad would have been so proud." His voice cracked when he said it, and I knew immediately that he was thinking about us as much as he was thinking about Jen's dad dying before she graduated. They weren't friends or anything, but all of our parents shared in our bond. When Jen's dad died, my father had been in shock for weeks.

"Yeah, he would've been."

"Carly, this cheating thing," my dad began. "I hope I never made you feel that going to Princeton meant that much—meant that you had to cheat to get there. If it happens, that's great; if it doesn't, that's fine, too."

I didn't say anything.

"Really, I mean it. I love you no matter what."

"Seriously?"

"Seriously."

Wow.

"Thanks, Dad. That means a lot." And it did. I walked over and gave him a kiss on the head. But much as I would've loved to have basked in that moment a little longer—I had to jet.

"I gotta run. Sorry Dad. I gotta catch the bus."

"Bus?" He coughed like I'd just told him I had three heads. "Where's Molly?"

I heard the whine of the school bus, so I just told him

it was a long story, grabbed my backpack, and flew out the front door.

At the corner I saw the bus idling, and I watched as Ronald stepped on. Even from a distance I could hear the chanting of *"Gross! Gross! Gross!"* and I waved like a maniac, hoping to catch the eye of the bus driver. He gestured that he would wait for me.

Like I said before, I'd be hard pressed to name any senior girls who took the bus—there definitely weren't any on Ronald's route—and as I neared, the pimply faces of freshman boys popped out of the windows. The yellow doors swung open, and even before I got on, there was on overture of underclassmen's whistles and catcalls. I suddenly wasn't as sure about this move as I had been the night before, and even the bus driver gave me a second look as I gazed at the stairwell; not a checking-me-out kind of look, but a why-in-the-hell-are-torturing-yourself-with-this kind of look.

But I was a girl on a mission, and I climbed the three black-and-green steps with gusto.

As I looked down the aisle, the hooting and hollering suddenly quieted down, and I swear you could've heard a pin drop. My name was whispered from seat to seat: "That's Carly Biels," and in my own head I heard a drumroll. A few of the younger girls made room for me, but there—midway back on the right—was Ronald. He was staring at me wide-eyed and baffled. I walked with my head high, directly to him.

"Can I sit with you, Mr. Gross?" I asked.

"Where's Molly?"

"I wanted to ride with you," I answered.

He squinted and then scooted over. "Okay."

We sat in silence for a while, and the driver ground the gears as we climbed Stepstone Hill Road. We passed Gordy's, and I thought of my conversation with Molly. Now everything with the Taker was behind me.

Feeling that the moment was right, I pulled out a piece of paper from my back pocket. I handed it to Ronald.

"I don't want your apology," he said.

"Just open it," I said, forcing it into his palm.

He unfolded the paper.

Question #1
In order for Ronald to forgive Carly for having been terrible to him, she needs to . . .
    (A) go to the prom with him
    (B) take him on a shopping spree at Abercrombie & Fitch

(C) sleep on his doorstep for five nights
in a row
(D) become his mother's best friend
(E) none of the above

Ronald uncapped a pen and circled *E*.

I looked away, crestfallen. So that was that.

"You don't need to do any of those things," he said. "Just be you—that's the way I like you."

"Really?"

He nodded, before smirking. "Although my mother would probably have preferred *D*."

"Yeah. I always got the feeling I occupied a special place in your mother's heart."

"She liked it that we were study partners."

"*Friends*," I corrected. "We're friends."

He looked at me carefully and then nodded.

"Yeah, friends."

We said nothing for a few moments.

"Did you really want to ride with me, or did Molly not show up?" he asked.

"Ronald. I wouldn't lie about this."

"No joke?"

And then I pulled a page from *his* book. "Just trust me."

He grinned and glanced out the window.

"So what do you say, Ronald? Can we study together again?"

He scratched his chin and looked at me playfully. I saw a sparkle of the Ronald of old. "Only if you take the Gross Method Oath."

"And what would that be?"

He raised his right hand, like in court. "Repeat after me: 'I shall not use any other method for as long as I live, so help me God, even if my father tells me to.'"

Ronald would always be a little dorky, wouldn't he? But then again—that was his charm. And there was so much more to life than being cool.

"Come on repeat it," he said in mock seriousness.

I laughed—and then said it.

And it was right about then that it happened. It started very low, in the back row. The kids on the bus were chanting something—I couldn't make it out exactly—and it grew louder and louder with every second. Suddenly, I realized what they were saying: "*Gross. Gross. Gross.*" But this time—and no doubt for the first time—they were pronouncing it the way Ronald's mom had always told them they should: like *floss*.

Try as he might, Ronald couldn't resist giving in to the

look of delight that was spreading across his face. The chanting kept going until the whole bus was shouting at the top of their lungs—"*Gross! Gross! Gross!*"—when at long last Ronald stood up and saluted the crowd, and every freshman and sophomore boy on bus 96 broke out in cheers and applause.

I'd never seen anyone look so happy.

BUT THE BUS RIDE was shaping up to be the best part of the day. Brad and I hadn't spoken since I'd seen him with Tori. He didn't know that I knew.

He did know something was wrong, though. He'd called three times last night about Rick. I didn't call him back, and at 11:30 P.M. he texted me three stars—our code for "very serious call immediately."

After we got off the bus, I left Ronald outside the main building of the school, and we agreed to meet in the lab at lunch. Instead of going to my locker, however, I headed right to American Lit., hoping to avoid Brad.

No such luck.

As I approached Mrs. G.'s room, I saw him. He was standing by the door with a strange look on his face. I

315

decided to play cool. I didn't want a scene in front of the whole school, and I just kept telling myself he didn't know what I knew.

"Hey," he said.

"Hey."

"What's wrong? Why are you ignoring me?"

When he spoke, my eyes stayed locked on his. I wanted to see what lying looked like. I wanted to see how little he cared for us.

"I'm not. I've been busy and I haven't had time to call you back," I said.

"You're lying," he hissed.

I was lying. That was rich. *J'accuse!*

I felt my emotional control unraveling, but I steeled myself. I wasn't going to cry over this jerk; at least not in front of him.

"Maybe."

"What's wrong with you—what's all this 'tude about?"

"I have an attitude? *I* have an attitude?"

"Yeah, you're not the only one getting jammed with the SAT—look how screwed Rick is now," he said.

"I'm not stressed about the SAT. I'm stressed because I saw your tongue down Tori's throat last night," I said as matter-of-factly as I could manage.

Brad's jaw dropped. His face whitened. He began stammering. I could see him searching his mind for a response that would right our tumbled world.

"I gotta go to class, Brad. I don't think there's anything to say."

"Wait," he rushed. "I'm sorry—it just happened. I love you. . . . It meant nothing."

"Nothing to you," I said, "but everything to me."

As I walked away, he grabbed my arm, but I jerked it free. Evidently aware of what was about to unfold, Mrs. G. came to the door and stood between us.

"Good-bye, Mr. Korian," she said, and calmly shut the door in his face.

I guess others had been watching us through the door as well, because as I walked into the classroom and glided down the aisle, it was dead silent. All eyes were on me. A couple of the girls mouthed "r u ok?" to me, but I didn't acknowledge their sympathies. I didn't acknowledge anyone.

I took my seat and took a deep breath. Up in the front of the room I saw Mrs. G. give me a little nod—a nod of support and approval—and, grudgingly, I smiled and nodded back. An instant later, she clapped her hands, grabbed her copy of *The Portrait of a Lady*, and cleared her throat.

"Who can tell me what Isabelle Archer saw when she looked into the fire in chapter forty-two?"

I looked around and saw all the clueless boys and vacant girls. I raised my hand.

"Carly."

"She saw every bad decision she'd ever made."

"Go on," Mrs. G. said.

"She saw herself for the first time—warts and all. I mean, she was conscious; the fire was a window to her soul, and for the first time she saw that Osmond was a fake, that he had never loved her."

"Yes!"

"And she was better for it—better because she knew what her mistake was all along," I added.

"Without question . . ." Mrs. G. said with a huge smile. ". . . Without question."

While Mrs. G. started asking other questions, I closed my eyes for a few minutes, listening to the banter of the class, and despite the heartache of it all, I knew Isabelle Archer wasn't the only young American girl who had made more than a few terrible decisions, and lived to tell about it.

I NEVER DID HEAR from the FBI. My correspondence with Mr. Lettich—aka the Taker—must never have surfaced, and I finally saw the point of his cryptic methods of communication. Like a death-row inmate who gets a last minute pardon from the governor, I swore myself to the straight-and-narrow path, and dedicated all my time to getting a good score on the SAT the old-fashioned way: through hard work.

With the final test date bearing down on us, the energy among the seniors who were retaking the SAT was manic as we made our final preparations for the test that would forever affect the course of our lives. Stressful, right? Knowing how much this exam meant—at least for those of us who needed to do better than we did the first time—

even the teachers lightened up on the relentless workload of homework so we could focus our energies on what was looming ever closer.

And if there was anyone who had a ton riding on this test . . . it was me.

I dreamed of the day when standardized tests would no longer be part of my life—hadn't this actually all begun in like, the second grade with the ERB or something?—but until that day, I resigned myself to the fate of a high school student. To make a long story short, I pretty much had no time for anyone or anything except for studying, and my life essentially consisted of living, breathing, and eating the SAT.

So much for the glamour of being seventeen.

Day in and day out, however, Ronald was there, guiding me through the process and cheering me on. By now you know enough about him that I don't have to get into the nitty-gritty of our studying methods—or his personality quirks—but just know . . . he was awesome. And the more I got to know him, the more I really began to believe that my original perceptions of him were wrong—except, of course, for his predilection (SAT word, look it up!) for bad clothes. All joking aside, I honestly don't know what I would've done without him. Out from underneath the useless teaching of Mr. Lettich, I finally felt like everything was moving in the right direction.

But to be totally honest, I still had the nagging fear that I might freeze up when it came time to take the exam. And then wouldn't all my work have been for nothing? I told my worries to Ronald, but he told me that I should just do the work and that with the confidence I found, all would be okay come test day.

But that, of course, remained to be seen.

The day before the big test, Ronald and I had our last tutoring session. Seated at my kitchen table, we did a huge review of everything that we'd studied, going through each section topic by topic. As we got to the end, I realized I was sad. Not sad that the SAT was going to be over—what a relief that was going to be!—but sad that this journey Ronald and I had made together was coming to a close. I'd certainly never expected to grow so close to him.

"So what else should I study tonight?" I asked as Ronald loaded his backpack.

"Absolutely nothing," he replied. "It'll only mess you up. Tonight, the best thing for you to do is not to even think about the SAT. You need to relax and just let it all go. Watch some TV, kick back. But go to bed early."

Not study at all? I wasn't so sure about this.

"Really? Maybe I'll come across something that'll be—"

He put up his palm to stop me talking.

"But shouldn't I—"

Palm.

"What—"

Palm!

I folded my arms and pouted playfully.

"Has the Gross ever steered you wrong before?"

I thought about it. He hadn't. And skeptical as I was, something told me that what Ronald was saying was true. Maybe I did need to relax.

It was right then that a thought jumped into my mind.

"I don't know if you have plans . . . but do you want to get some ice cream at the diner?" I asked.

"When?"

"Now."

Ronald looked up at me and cocked his head to the side. "Really?"

"Sure. My treat."

He smiled and slung his bag over his shoulder. "Take us to warp speed."

When we reached the diner, the parking lot was

hopping with kids from Guilford and nearby Pinewood. Apparently not everyone was going to be facing the dreaded bubble sheets tomorrow.

It was as we waited on line at the outside window, however, that I realized that maybe this had been a mistake. Off to the side, a bunch of the lacrosstitutes were horsing around, arm wrestling, and chewing tobacco. One of them spotted me with Ronald and pointed over our way. I turned away, but it was too late.

"What's the matter?" Ronald asked.

"Nothing," I answered, forcing a smile.

For the next couple of minutes everything was fine, but just as we were getting ready to leave, Rick Sorenson—OMG, wasn't he in prison or something yet?!—slithered up to where we were standing.

"Well, well, well, what have we here?" he said.

"Take a hike, Rick, we're not in the mood," I warned, hoping he'd hit the road.

"Carly Biels and Ronald Gross!" he announced so that everyone within earshot could hear. I wasn't sure, but I thought I smelled beer on his breath.

"So is this like, a date?" he asked.

"Shouldn't you be in juvie?" I retorted.

He ignored my jab.

"Look, everybody! Carly Biels is out with the Gross Man himself."

Next to me, I felt Ronald tense up. For the umpteenth time in his life, Ronald found himself as the butt of a joke. But this time—for the first time—*I* was going to do the right thing.

"That's right, Rick," I said with assurance as I hooked my arm through Ronald's. "I'm out with Ronald Gross. Can we all just grow up now?"

Out of the corner of my eye, I saw Ronald stand just a little bit taller, and I gave his arm a pat. There were some whispers among the crowd. Rick was thrown by my acknowledgment, but clearly he wasn't going to be put off.

"You know, Gross Man," Rick spat as he moved toward Ronald, "you and I still have some unfinished business. I know you gave me up to the police."

I pushed Ronald behind me.

"Knock it off, Rick. You're drunk."

"Ooohhh, look at Carly protecting her new boyfriend! How quickly she forgets our boy Brad!"

"I'm not Brad's property. We broke up, you idiot."

"Duh," he mocked. "Maybe if you'd put out he wouldn't have had to go lookin' for some elsewhere."

With that he laughed and turned to a bunch of the

lacrosse guys behind him, and they high-fived, hearty chuckling all around.

To my surprise, Ronald moved out from behind me and stepped toward Rick.

"That's enough," Ronald commanded.

Um . . . what was he doing?

Everyone went deadly silent. Slowly . . . very slowly . . . Rick turned around.

"I'm sorry. Did you say something, Gross?"

"Yeah," Ronald declared, his fists clenching at his side.

Rick looked at him carefully, then snorted. "Get a load of this, guys," he jeered to his crew. "Nerd Dick here is standing up for his frigid girlfriend."

"Shut. Up." Ronald said.

And that was the moment I saw Rick get mad.

I went up behind Ronald and whispered in his ear. "Don't do this, Ronald. Let's just go home. Please."

But he shook his head. He was determined to stand his ground.

I was flattered that Ronald wanted to defend my honor and all, but this was bad. Really bad. Rick was a big guy, and Ronald was maybe a hundred and forty-five pounds soaking wet. This wouldn't be a fight. It would be a slaughter.

Rick stalked up to Ronald so they were face-to-face.

Well, actually Ronald's face to Rick's chest.

"I'm about to give you a beating like you've never had in your life, Gross."

In a last hope of averting certain disaster—and bloodshed—I tried to wedge myself between them, but Rick shoved me out of the way. He didn't push me too hard, but I guess my heel caught in a crack in the pavement or something, because next thing I knew I was falling backward. Thinking I had been assaulted, Ronald flashed into action, and with a high-pitched banshee scream, flung himself on Rick. From the ground I saw Ronald—looking like some crazed monkey—with his arms clenched around Rick's shoulders and neck, trying to wrestle him to the ground. A moment later, Rick broke Ronald's clutch and tossed him onto the hood of a nearby car. Over the shouts of the guy whose car was getting dented, Rick threw a punch at Ronald's face, but missed as Ronald somehow managed to roll off the hood to the ground and onto his feet.

Now the two were hunched over, squaring off, ready to unleash more blows. While they circled, trying to find the right move, kids huddled on either side—the jocks cheering Rick, and the lesser lights of the Guilford social world rooting for Ronald. Suddenly, Rick surged forward, and poor

Ronald—probably never having been in a fight in his life—was caught off guard, and Rick drove him backward off his feet and onto the ground in a veritable demonstration of a textbook football tackle. With Ronald now on his back, Rick used his knees to pin Ronald's hands, and a moment later, Ronald was defenseless, with Rick straddling his chest. Like a caught animal, he tried to get out, but it was impossible, and no one would help him. It was too awful. Revving up for the pain he was about to inflict, Rick breathed in deep and cocked his hand far back behind his head, ready to rain down the blow to end all blows on Ronald's head.

I tried to get to my feet to help him—somewhere a girl shrieked in horror—and in slow motion I saw Rick's hand begin to move downward toward Ronald's wide frightened eyes.

No!

But it was right then, with a speed so blazing that it didn't seem human, I saw what looked like a shadow fly across the parking lot and catch Rick's fist midblow before it could land, and suddenly Rick's body was flying up and off of Ronald.

"What the fuck!" I heard Rick cry as he rolled into the metal bumper of a car.

At first I thought Ronald had kicked him off. But it was then, underneath the blue neon sign of the diner, that I saw who it was.

Brad.

"Lock it up, Rick!" Brad shouted.

But Rick got up and strode over to Brad. "Get out of my way, Korian," Rick spat like a wild animal.

Brad stuck his nose in Rick's face. "I'll be *first*. You want Gross—you come through me."

Rick gritted his teeth, readying himself to make a go of it with Brad. Everyone's jaws dropped open. Even the jocks went silent. It was one thing to pick on Ronald Gross, but it was quite another to get into it with Brad. Despite everything, Brad was still *the man* at Guilford High.

Brad stood his ground, chin high in the air, while Rick eyed him with menace. Then, a second later—as if thinking better of it—Rick stepped back away from Brad.

"What the hell is wrong with you, Korian?"

"You know what?" Brad said. "You're a real jackass."

The lacrosse guys who had been cheering for Rick now laughed at his expense (they all kowtowed to whoever was biggest, after all), and Rick—clearly bested—took off defeated into the night. Brad turned to Ronald and helped him to his feet.

"Thanks," Ronald said.

"It's cool," Brad replied with neither kindness nor animosity. "I owed you one."

Sensing the show was over, the crowd began to dissipate. Even though Ronald would've been soundly beaten, a bunch of guys I recognized from the debate team came over and started patting him on the back and telling him how great he was for standing up to Rick.

Brad headed off toward his SUV, which still idled in one of the rows, and once I'd made sure Ronald was okay, I jogged after him.

"Brad!"

He turned and faced me.

"Thanks," I said, remembering why it was I'd dated him for so long. Somewhere deep down he had an unerring compass of right and wrong. "That was big of you."

He looked away, and grimaced. He was silent for a few beats. "Look, Carly. I'm really sorry about what happened. . . ." He hesitated. "With me and Tori."

The apology caught me totally off guard.

"These last two weeks have been awful for me," he continued, genuinely pained. "I haven't been able to think about anything else but you. I know how bad I messed up. I'm so sorry. Really."

"There's nothing to say about it, Brad. You did what you did and that's all there is to it," I replied.

"Can't you forgive me?"

"And like, what? Get back together?" I asked gently.

"Well—yeah."

"Brad. You'd been hooking up with someone else for weeks while we were going out. Do you know how humiliating that was?"

"I know, I know. I was stupid."

Brad grew quiet and stared at the ground.

Over his shoulder, I saw Ronald turn in our direction. When he saw Brad and me talking so seriously, his grin faded.

"I took you for granted," Brad whispered. "But try not to think about what happened with Tori. Think about what we had before then, the fun times we had together. There were some good ones, weren't there?"

I didn't immediately answer him, but after a moment I nodded.

"Can't we give it another try?"

Maybe we could make a go of it again, I thought. Couldn't I just forget about Tori and focus on what we did have together? Hadn't we been terribly in love at one point? And yet, there was Ronald—still watching us—the boy who had opened a whole new world to me.

At that moment it was more than I could deal with.

"Brad, I just don't know," I finally answered. "I can't even really think about this—I have the biggest test of my life tomorrow, and until that's done, I can't give you an answer. Okay?"

Brad said nothing, but then nodded. "That's cool. I'm willing to wait."

When I got home that night I looked at the stack of books on my desk, an assortment of SAT study guides that I'd never use again. I picked them up and dropped them into the garbage.

I opened my window and breathed in the cold night air. Ronald's light was on, but his shades were closed. Tomorrow would determine what the rest of my life would be like. That's what they wanted me to think, anyway. I closed the window, put on my PJs, took out my diary, and climbed into bed. I wrote the following:

SAT Question

Who should Carly choose to spend the rest of her high school life with?

(A) Brad

(B) Ronald

(C) None of the above

(D) She's glad she doesn't have to answer this one tomorrow

If Carly were to _____ the SAT, she would be _____ for life.

    (A) ace . . . set

    (B) miss . . . humiliated

    (C) fail . . . home

    (D) eat . . . sick

    (E) blow . . . screwed

SO THERE I WAS—just like I had been ten weeks before—perched on the edge of my bed with my finger on the speed dial. This was it. Time to find out if all my studying had paid off.

I was about to get my scores.

But I had to wait a little longer. It was only 7:58 A.M.

When I took the SAT for the second time, I felt really good about how it went. Sure, I was still a total stress case on my way to the test—and watching some girl I didn't know have a hysterical meltdown in the hallway before the exam didn't help things—but this time, once the proctor handed out the booklets, I got in my own zone and made it happen. Yes, there were some tough questions, but there wasn't a single one that I hadn't seen some variation of while working with Ronald, and minute after minute, problem after problem, I simply used the approaches that Ronald had taught me and stayed focused. I had no idea of course if I'd gotten any of them right—are you ever totally sure when you take a test?—but there definitely weren't any questions that had left me completely lost.

What was coolest, however, was that I never got wound up—I never freaked out during the test. Remember how I used to freeze up during standardized tests? Well, this time I didn't. Whether it was because I'd done so much work with Ronald, or I'd shucked off all the pressure that I'd allowed other people to put on me during these big things—like my parents and Brad—I'm not sure. All I know is that I kept it together the whole time—and that in itself was a big achievement.

7:59 A.M.

I wonder what Ronald's doing right now.

With college applications looming and a mountain of work that I'd put off while prepping for the SAT, Ronald and I hadn't done much together after our night at the diner. That's not to say we weren't keeping in touch—I saw him on the bus every morning, after all, and we talked on the phone a lot at night—but I was looking forward to having more free time so we could hang out again. I didn't know where things were going to end up. Brad or Ronald, Ronald or Brad. I just kept pushing the question aside, focusing on smaller matters—the solvable ones.

As if sensing that I was thinking about him, suddenly there he was, across the street, standing in the window of his room waving to me. I waved back, and he pointed to his watch. He gave me a thumbs-up.

8:00 A.M.

Let's do it.

I rose to my feet and hit speed dial.

"Thank you for calling the College Board," the recorded voice answered. "If you are a student, press one. If . . ."

I went through the menu before punching in my ID and PIN numbers.

"Your scores are as follows," the automated voice began. "Writing . . . 710."

Okay . . . same as last time.

"Critical Reading . . . 700."

Gooooood.

"Math . . . 790."

790?! I got a 790 on the math?

I did it. I DID IT!

I couldn't help myself; I started jumping up and down and screaming for joy. Probably thinking I was being murdered or something, my parents ran into my room. I could barely put two words together to tell them my scores, but somehow I managed, and needless to say, they were ecstatic. Pretty soon they were jumping up and down, too—even my dad. My mother started crying out of joy.

I quickly looked out my window to see if Ronald was still there, but he had disappeared.

"Listen, I'll be right back. I want to go tell Ronald!"

"Of course! Of course!" my father replied, before hugging my mother in happiness-cum-relief.

I grabbed my cell from the bedside table so I could text the Sistas on my way across the street, and took off down the steps. Just as I reached the front door, my phone beeped with an incoming message. Maybe it was Ronald wanting to know how I did.

I opened it . . . and went pale.

CALLER UNKNOWN: Are you satisfied? Time for payback.
Meet me at the mall in four hours.

—The Taker

Oh. My. God.

SLUMPED ON MY FRONT STEPS, I stared at my phone. So this was it. This was how my story was going to end. There aren't words to describe what I felt at that moment. Shock, woe, horror, abject fear—they're all too inadequate, too weak. Someone once said that terrible things happen very quickly, and this text fell into that category; it was like getting hit by a car and struck by lightning at the same time.

But how did this happen? How could it be that after Jen's investigation, the Guilford cops, the state police, and the FBI—he was still out there? So the Taker wasn't Lettich? Wasn't Rick Sorenson? Wasn't the Terminator? Who, then? Only the most devious of people, I answered myself. Someone who in spite of it all, even after all the arrests had gone down, had managed to find a way to dodge the FBI and have the nerve to go through with it. He wasn't a person to be swayed from what he wanted, and I recognized that, given my current circumstances, that was not a good thing.

Not only had all my studying been in vain—the endless nights huddled over my books, the parties skipped, the friendships endangered—but those scores that I had been so overjoyed to call my own were *not* mine. Like a professional athlete caught using steroids, all my records would have asterisks by them (at least in my book). I'd never know how well I would've done if I'd stood on my own. And even though I believed I could've gotten those scores myself—I hadn't. I was a fraud. A failure. A liar.

But I was also in danger. The Taker's demand that I meet him at the mall at noon summoned only the worst images to mind. Remember my nightmare? Well I was picturing things far, far worse. Much as I wanted to cut and run before having to face this almost certain . . . (I don't even want to say the words, so I won't) . . . how could I not show up? If I didn't he would expose me, and I would fall into the same camp as those people who had so recently been disgraced and paraded on the front page of the *New York Times*. Would I want my name to live on in black infamy? If it were just me, I probably could've lived with it. But I couldn't do it to my parents. What was done was done. I had to pay the price for my actions.

"So how'd you do?"

I looked up and there was Ronald loping across the street toward me. *Oh, no.* I covered my face with my hands—I couldn't even bear to look him in the eye.

"Oh, they couldn't have been that bad," he said. "I just don't believe it."

"Please, Ronald," I said into my hands. "Please, just go away."

He put his hand on my back. "Just tell me."

What was I supposed to say to him? Was I supposed to tell him that all the hours he'd spent tutoring me were pointless? That would've been worse than having done poorly, because at least it would've been my work on those bubble sheets. He'd be crushed.

"Cars," he went on. "Just talk to me."

I needed to think. To be clearheaded. I had to figure out how I was going to go through with what I had to do—but also how I was going to live with myself afterward. I wished and wished that it was just a nightmare—that I would wake up seconds from now and, though shaken, be thankful that it had been only a dream. But with my nails digging into my palms, I couldn't wake up—because this was no dream.

I felt a confident hand on my shoulder before another gently pulled my hands from my face. I opened my eyes, blinking through the sun, and there was Ronald's face right in front of mine.

"What is it?" he asked.

"I got a 2200."

He jumped to his feet. "Carly, that's awesome!!"

"No, no, no." I made him sit down. "It's all so screwed up."

"How? That's great!"

"They're not mine."

"What do you mean?"

"I hired someone to take the test for me."

He sat up super straight and visibly edged away.

"What are you talking about?"

"He took the test for me . . ."

"Who's *he*?"

". . . and now I have to go see him at the mall and give him whatever he asks for," I cried. "I'm so scared, Ronald. I'm so incredibly freaked."

I buried my face in my hands again and couldn't see how Ronald reacted to the news. He didn't say anything, though—just dead silence. I'm sure he was thinking I was the most despicable person in the world.

"You can't just not show up?" he asked.

I shook my head.

"That sucks."

"Yeah."

Ronald pushed himself to his feet and wiped off the back of his pants. I figured he was getting ready to tell me that he never wanted to see me again.

"I'll go with you," he said.

I looked up at him and saw the boy I'd known puff up into a knight.

"You can't—I don't want that."

"I will," he said. "And that's that."

I wanted to say no, but how could I? I was scared. I needed somebody there just in case things went really bad. But never—not in my wildest dreams—had I imagined that my hero in a time of need would be Ronald Gross.

"Okay . . . and thank you."

At twelve o'clock, I rolled down the window of my dad's car and took the ticket to go into the parking lot. Behind me, Ronald lay hidden stealthily in the footwell of the backseat—hardly in a comfortable position, but with me nonetheless. Our drive to the mall together had been pretty awkward. While Ronald had been willing to come along to see this through, when I tried to tell him about how it had all begun with the Taker, how he'd contacted me, how we'd first met, etcetera, etcetera, Ronald said he didn't want to know anything about it. Who could blame him? Even though he was there with me as a friend, I'm sure he resented me for having done this, and I realized that my having the Taker ace the SAT for me was the biggest betrayal yet. I told him over and over that I'd tried to end it with the Taker—that I'd even sent him that e-mail firing him—but I don't know if Ronald believed me. Then again, it probably didn't matter. I'm sure that as far as he was concerned, I was simply a cheater. 'Cause I was.

We circled down lower and lower in the parking lot, like we were gradually descending into hell. The last of the cars for shoppers and employees at the mall that day were parked in the third basement. After that it was empty. There was no chance that anyone would be around where I was meeting the Taker on level six.

Like last time, I counted the numbers until I got to space 698 and backed in. The light in the corner between the pillar and the deck above was still burned out, and I suspected that there, deep in the shadows, he was waiting.

There was no telltale sign of the cigarette lighting, but the clock on the dash now read 12:04 P.M. The Taker didn't strike me as the type of person to arrive late.

I covered my mouth like I was coughing. "If you hear me scream you know what to do."

"Roll down my window so I can hear more clearly," Ronald whispered back.

Good thinking.

I did and then got out.

With a fear bordering on hysteria, I began walking toward the darkness, ready to receive my sentence. Sure I wasn't going to the gas chamber, but I grasped what it must be like to be on death row, makeing that last walk. I said a silent prayer in my head and just hoped that my legs would get me there.

But when I crossed from the light into the shadows, and my eyes adjusted . . . I realized that there was no one waiting. Just some empty beer bottles piled haphazardly. Then I noticed something else. There was a book lying conspicuously open on the ground with a passage highlighted. I picked it up and read it.

. . . when Woodward had an inquiry to make, he would move the flowerpot with the red flag to the balcony. . . .

I noticed that there was a different page marked with a Post-it, and yet again there was another passage highlighted.

. . . he and Woodward would meet in a predesignated underground parking garage. . . .

Huh.

I flipped the cover shut to see what it was. *All the President's Men.* This was strange. Not what I was expecting at all. Was this some new game the Taker was playing with me, or was he just showing me where he had found his methods? But why would he do that? *All the President's Men. All the President's Men?* Wasn't there someone I knew who had been reading this book? I quickly checked the flyleaf, and sure enough there was the stamp:

Property of Guilford High School

Who was it? Who had been reading this book?

And just as I remembered who it was—the image from that very day I'd bombed the SAT suddenly clear in my mind's eye—I turned around. There he was, leaning against the hood of my car.

RONALD!!

"It's you?" I yelled.

Ronald shrugged his shoulders. But if I'd imagined that the Taker was going to be menacing and demanding, Ronald had never looked more shy and apologetic.

I strode over to him. "You're the Taker."

"First rule of the Taker is . . ." But before he could finish, I slapped him across his face.

"How could you? You jerk!"

"What?" he stuttered, confused.

I started walking away from the car.

"I just wanted to help you," he called after me.

"Help?" I said as I spun around on him. "Stalking me is help? Sending creepy messages is help?"

"I didn't mean it that way."

"And then to take the test for me after building me up . . . How could you, Ronald?!"

"I didn't take the test."

"What?"

"I was just bluffing," he explained. "That was just to get you to study with me."

I struggled to process this latest revelation.

"So they're my scores?"

He nodded.

He didn't take the test for me. I'd gotten the great score myself.

Needless to say, part of me was relieved (and overjoyed) to know that the scores were mine again. But I soon realized that I didn't care. I was over the SAT. I may have aced the aptitude test, but Ronald had flunked the decency test. Just like Brad, he had deceived me. Lied to me. *How could he?*

A tear burned my cheek.

Ronald saw my reaction and looked away, his face crinkling in pain.

"Before everyone got their scores back, Mrs. G. and I talked about students who might need help at the tutorial lab, and your name came up. We both knew that you could do well, but that you had a habit of freezing up. And that's when I thought of it. I figured maybe if you weren't so stressed about the SAT, that if you thought it was all taken care of, that you would relax and do as well as you were capable of doing."

Unlike Brad—I reasoned with myself—Ronald had meant well. He was just inept. But that didn't excuse things. On the other hand, what if Ronald had held all my sins against him in *his* heart—hadn't he forgiven me time and time again? And besides, had the Taker actually been real, wouldn't I have been begging Ronald to overlook what I'd done? To take me for the person I was?

"I'm sorry," he said. "I didn't realize it would upset you so much."

"So you were never going to take the test for me?"

He shook his head.

"And that's how it all began? That's it?" I pushed, still feeling like I hadn't gotten the whole story out of him.

"And . . . you know . . . I was sort of hoping we'd end up studying together." He trailed off, struggling to explain himself. "I've lived across the street from you for ten years, and up until the last eight weeks, you've never said more than five words to me. You were *Carly Biels*, and I was Ronald Gross" (pronounced like you'd think it would be). "I hoped that maybe if you spent a little time with me, you might see me as someone other than dork-boy."

He paused, but I said nothing.

"Truth is . . . I just wanted to get to sit next to you. Even for an hour. Because you've always been the girl of my dreams."

The girl of his dreams. No one had ever said that to me before. With five words, those five little words, I melted like last winter's snow. I think the SAT word would be "swooned."

He glumly reached into his pocket. "Here's your charm bracelet back."

I stared down at it: the bracelet that Brad had given me.

And in that instant my heart made the decision that my mind hadn't been able to answer.

"I never did like lacrosse," I said.

Ronald raised an eyebrow.

"You can never lie to me again," I said, looking him in the eye. "Just promise, swear that you'll always be honest with me from now on."

He nodded. And I believed him.

"Don't just nod," I demanded, poking him in the chest. "Say, 'I'll always be honest with you.'"

"I'll always be honest with you."

"Ma'am!"

Ronald smiled, catching on. "I will always be honest with you . . . ma'am!"

As soon as he finished, I put my arms around him, and there, where it had all begun, I gave him the kiss of his dreams. And I'm not sure if Ronald had ever kissed a girl before, but he certainly didn't need any training. It was electric!

When we broke from our embrace, Ronald staggered back a little and leaned against the car.

"Wow."

I giggled and tousled his hair. "But I do have some bad news."

"What?"

"I'm demoting you back to *Ronnie*."

THE END

If you finish before time is called, you may check your work on this section only.
Do not turn to any other section.